W9-CAD-697

Carey Cove Midwives

Delivering babies around the clock at Christmastime!

It's Christmas in Carey Cove, a bustling seaside town on the stunning Cornish coastline, where a team of dedicated midwives are poised to deliver long-awaited bundles of joy, day and night! While decorations are going up, fairy lights are being turned on and Santa is doing the rounds, these midwives are busy doing exactly what they do best wherever they're most needed. But could this magical festive season with mistletoe pinned up around every corner also be the perfect opportunity for the staff of Carey House to follow their hearts... and finally find love?

Don't be late for these special deliveries with...

Christmas with the Single Dad Doc
by Annie O'Neil

Festive Fling to Forever
by Karin Baine

Both available now.

And look out for

Christmas Miracle on Their Doorstep
by Ann McIntosh

Single Mom's Mistletoe Kiss
by Rachel Dove

Available next month.

Dear Reader,

As always, I'm thrilled to be part of a Christmas continuity alongside some amazing authors. We get to create our own little festive hub full of interesting characters and drama for our readers to enjoy and we get to call it work.

I have to admit I'm very like my heroine, Sophie. I'm not one to take unnecessary risks. Although, if there was a hot paramedic like Roman Callahan involved, I might be persuaded to jump off a cliff, too!

There's nothing like the return of her old childhood crush to make Sophie reassess her life and wonder how it could have turned out if she hadn't kissed Roman and scared him out of the village for ten years. Now that he's back for the Christmas holidays, and there's a mutual attraction, she thinks she can get closure with a no-strings fling. However, it only brings them closer than ever. A problem for commitment-phobic Roman!

Hopefully, the couple's roller-coaster ride over the festive period will make you feel Christmassy and keep you hooked on all the adventures happening in Carey Cove.

Enjoy!

Karin x

FESTIVE FLING TO FOREVER

KARIN BAINE

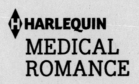

MEDICAL
ROMANCE

If you purchased this book without a cover you should be aware
that this book is stolen property. It was reported as "unsold and
destroyed" to the publisher, and neither the author nor the
publisher has received any payment for this "stripped book."

Special thanks and acknowledgment are given to Karin Baine
for her contribution to the Carey Cove Midwives miniseries.

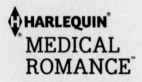

HARLEQUIN®
MEDICAL
ROMANCE™

Recycling programs
for this product may
not exist in your area.

ISBN-13: 978-1-335-73745-8

Festive Fling to Forever

Copyright © 2022 by Harlequin Enterprises ULC

All rights reserved. No part of this book may be used or reproduced in
any manner whatsoever without written permission except in the case of
brief quotations embodied in critical articles and reviews.

This is a work of fiction. Names, characters, places and incidents
are either the product of the author's imagination or are used fictitiously.
Any resemblance to actual persons, living or dead, businesses,
companies, events or locales is entirely coincidental.

For questions and comments about the quality of this book,
please contact us at CustomerService@Harlequin.com.

Harlequin Enterprises ULC
22 Adelaide St. West, 41st Floor
Toronto, Ontario M5H 4E3, Canada
www.Harlequin.com

Printed in U.S.A.

Karin Baine lives in Northern Ireland with her husband, two sons and her out-of-control notebook collection. Her mother and her grandmother's vast collection of books inspired her love of reading and her dream of becoming a Harlequin author. Now she can tell people she has a *proper* job! You can follow Karin on Twitter, @karinbaine1, or visit her website for the latest news—karinbaine.com.

Books by Karin Baine

Harlequin Medical Romance

Pups that Make Miracles
Their One-Night Christmas Gift

Single Dad Docs
The Single Dad's Proposal

Their One-Night Twin Surprise
Healed by Their Unexpected Family
Reunion with His Surgeon Princess
One Night with Her Italian Doc
The Surgeon and the Princess
The Nurse's Christmas Hero
Wed for Their One Night Baby
A GP to Steal His Heart

Visit the Author Profile page
at Harlequin.com for more titles.

For Josephine. Now reunited with Paddy xx

**Praise for
Karin Baine**

"Emotionally enchanting! The story was fast-
paced, emotionally charged and oh so satisfying!"
—*Goodreads* on *Their One-Night Twin Surprise*

CHAPTER ONE

THIS WAS AS adventurous as Sophie French liked to get. Actually, even being here on the jetty waving off Clem the boatman and Jack Matthews was a tad out of her comfort zone. Enys Island might only be across that stretch of water Jack was sailing over to get supplies but it wasn't Carey Cove and she didn't like to stray too far from home.

'See you later,' she called hopefully into the wind. It was Jack's pregnant wife she was here to see, otherwise she would never have ventured to somewhere so isolated in this weather. Her job as a midwife at Carey House meant she sometimes had to travel to the more remote areas around Cornwall to see her patients but putting herself in any jeopardy was not in her nature. If not for the sake of her patients she would happily stay put in her hometown for the rest of her days. Given the chance, she would have all of her

pregnant ladies safe and sound in the maternity ward at their cottage hospital lest anything happened, but not everyone thought as
she did. Some mothers-to-be preferred the
idea of a home birth, praying they would
have a perfect, natural delivery. There was
no reason they shouldn't, but Sophie liked
to be prepared for all emergencies.

She had always been a cautious child.
Much to her parents' chagrin, she was sure,
when they had the kind of adventurous spirit
she'd never possessed. Whilst they had trav-
elled the world on a shoestring budget, Sophie had been content to stay at home under
the care of her grandmother. As a young
girl, all she had craved was the security of
four walls and familiar surroundings over
snow-capped mountains and humid tropi-
cal forests. Things had not changed in her
twenty-nine years. Especially when her fears
had been proven tragically correct.

Only once, when she was ten years old,
had she tried to convince everyone, including herself, that she was ready to travel with
them. Only to get cold feet at the last minute
and disappoint everyone. Her guilt was further compounded when they'd been killed in
a mountaineering accident on that very trip.

Since then she had become what some

people called overcautious, but she only wanted to keep herself and her patients safe. Her one nod to her parents' legacy was her chosen career. After discovering her mother had trained as a midwife herself before quitting to travel, Sophie had followed in her footsteps to nearby Carey House.

Now a midwife herself, Sophie went on the journey along with her pregnant patients. Including home visits to isolated islands in wintry weather.

She hoisted her bag onto her shoulder and pulled her scarf up around her nose before facing into the wind. It was a short walk to the cottage but the weather and rocky terrain would make it a challenge. The land was mostly used for grazing and it was not conducive for sightseeing or travelling medical professionals.

The warm glow in the window up ahead and the cosy prospect of a home fire burning spurred Sophie onwards. She would never have survived her parents' Bohemian lifestyle, not knowing where or when she would next find shelter or food. Sometimes she wondered if she had been swapped at birth when she was so different to the people she had been born to. Perhaps there was a quiet, unassuming family out there somewhere, struggling to relate to their free-spirited daughter, who did not fit into their world either.

Sophie rapped on the door out of courtesy, even though she knew it would be unlocked. There was no need to worry about anyone breaking in on the island when the majority of the inhabitants were livestock. The Matthews could see everyone who visited Enys from the window of their front room.

'Hey, Molly. It's Sophie, the midwife from Carey House.'

'Hi, Sophie, come on in. It'll take me ages to haul my backside up out of bed to let you in otherwise,' the voice shouted from upstairs.

Usually Molly was already up doing her chores when Sophie got here, even with only a matter of weeks left of her pregnancy. To find her apparently still in bed was not like her at all.

Sophie hustled upstairs to the bedroom where she had done Molly's previous pregnancy checks. The room was dark, the curtains unopened and Molly was lying flat on the bed. She hadn't even managed to sit up for her visitor.

'Do you mind if I open the curtains for some light so I can see what I'm doing?'

'Go ahead,' Molly replied, mid-yawn.

'How are you feeling today?' Even in the gloom of the afternoon Sophie could see how pale and weary she looked. Not at all her usual vibrant, blooming self.

'Exhausted. I think it's the time of year. The darker days and horrible weather always make me feel tired.'

'Well, I'll just do a few checks to make sure there's nothing else going on. I'll go and give my hands a wash first, if that's okay?'

'Sure.' Molly attempted to hoist herself up and Sophie hooked a hand under her arm to help her into a sitting position. She propped up the pillows for Molly before going to wash in the bathroom.

'Not long to go now,' Sophie commented on her return, the thought of bringing another life into the world putting a smile on her face.

'Thank goodness. At this rate I think I could pass as Father Christmas if you put me in a red suit and beard.'

Sophie chuckled. It was always the same when her patients were late into their third trimester. As much as they were looking forward to the arrival of their little bundles of joy, they were also glad to get back control of their bodies.

Sophie had not experienced pregnancy for herself—perhaps one day if she was lucky—but she had dealt with enough pregnant women to witness their frustration and some of the more challenging aspects of childbearing.

'At least the little one will be here in time for Christmas to make it extra special.' The picture of a happy family gathered together always brought a lump to her throat. It was something she had never really had with her parents. They'd usually spent the winter months in exotic climes, leaving her with her grandmother for Christmas. As much as she had loved her gran, she'd longed to experience the kind of family get-togethers normal families had at that time of year. A quiet turkey dinner for two and the prospect of unwrapping a travel journal or some Peruvian panpipes did not hold the same excitement factor everyone else seemed to have leading up to the big day.

'Yes, I have all the present shopping done so I'm fully expecting not to leave the house once Jack brings the other supplies home. I will be happy with just the three of us cosied up in the cottage for Christmas.' There was a twinkle in Molly's eye as she said it. Highlighting to Sophie once more that the season was about being with family and loved ones, not token gifts or a desire to be somewhere warmer or more exciting than Carey Cove. That ache in her heart hurt a bit more.

'Sounds lovely.'

'Hopefully I'll be able to shake off this malaise or I won't be fit to even push this baby out when the time comes.'

'Don't worry. It will do you good to put your feet up for a while. I'm sure that lovely husband of yours will do anything you need.'

'Yes, I'm very lucky. He's been doing all the cooking. Not so good at the cleaning, but he's been a great help.'

'That's what I like to hear—a husband who isn't afraid to muck in when called upon. It makes life easier if there are two parents actively involved in the household. Now, I'm going to take a look at your blood pressure to make sure there's nothing else making you tired.' Sophie took out the cuff, wrapped it around Molly's arm and took the reading. Low blood pressure was common during pregnancy, but any significant drop could be a sign of something more serious, so it was necessary to keep a good record.

'Have you experienced any dizziness,

blurred vision or excessive thirst?' The symptoms most associated with low blood pressure.

'No. As I said, I'm just sleepy today.'

'That all seems fine,' Sophie said, undoing the cuff again, satisfied there was not a problem to worry about where her blood pressure was concerned. 'Do you have a urine sample for me?'

'It's there on the dresser.' Molly pointed over at the plastic sample bottle propped up on the dressing table.

Using the test strips from her bag, Sophie noted the results. 'Absolutely perfect. While I'm here I'll check on baby's progress too. If you could shuffle back down the bed that would be great.'

With Sophie's assistance Molly was able to lie down in order for her examination.

'I'll try and warm my hands up first,' she said, rubbing her hands together as Molly lifted her nightdress up over her sizeable bump.

Applying firm pressure, Sophie felt around, trying to gauge the baby's position. With five weeks to go she would have expected the baby to be moving freely but it soon became apparent the head was already engaged in the pelvis.

It wasn't completely unheard of and didn't mean there would be a problem or even that Molly would go into labour immediately. However, the baby remained in the occipito-posterior position, facing towards the stomach instead of the back, spine parallel to the mother's. Most babies would spontaneously rotate to face the right direction before birth, but on those rare occasions when the baby did not rotate there could be a prolonged delivery and severe backache where an epidural was needed to alleviate the pain. It could mean a hospital stay and she would prefer a transfer to St Isolde's, the main hospital in the area which dealt with their high-risk pregnancies.

'Is something wrong?' Molly queried when Sophie took her time confirming what was happening.

'Nothing to worry about, but your little one is facing the wrong way at the minute. There's plenty of time for him or her to turn around. Sometimes it can happen right at the last minute. I know you want a home birth, but a hospital delivery is something we might have to think about if things don't change.'

She could see the news had made Molly more emotional than usual, her eyes well-ing up with tears. It was understandable. Sophie wanted all of her patients to experience the birth process whatever way they envisioned it, it being such a special time in a mother's life. However, she had to put their welfare first.

'I would want Jack with me.'

'Of course. We don't need to make any decisions yet, just keep an eye on baby's position.'

With that, the mobile phone sitting on the night stand began to buzz.

'Speak of the devil.' Molly smiled and stretched across to answer it.

Sophie watched her smile transform into a frown before she handed the phone over to her. 'Jack wants to speak to you.'

'Hello? This is Sophie.'

'Sophie, I was hoping you could break the news to Molly... I don't want her to panic.'

Sophie's stomach plummeted into her shoes, waiting for the bad news to follow. Whatever it was, on top what she had just told her it was liable to send Molly into a tailspin, and she didn't need any further upset.

'Uh-huh?' She tried not to worry Molly, who was listening intently to every word, her forehead lined with concern.

'There's a storm rolling in. The weather changed so quickly Clem doesn't think we're going to be able to get back tonight.'

Sophie was momentarily stunned into silence as she processed the implications of what he was saying. Not only did it mean she couldn't get Molly to hospital if needed, but she wouldn't be getting home either. They were stranded here for the night.

'Okay. Let me know when that changes.' She made the decision not to share her concerns about the baby's position with him. There was nothing to say Molly would go into labour tonight and they could deal with that tomorrow, getting her a referral to St Isolde's. As usual, she was probably being overcautious, but it was better to be safe than sorry.

For now, the best she could do was keep her patient calm and ride out the storm with her.

Sophie watched the ominous grey sky from the kitchen window as she tackled the mountain of dirty dishes in the sink. Molly's fatigue and Jack's inability to keep up with the household chores meant she had something to keep her busy, to stop her mind wandering into the worst-case scenario now they were completely cut off from the mainland. It would be scary enough for two women alone in the house with a storm raging outside and the possibility of losing power without her imagination making matters worse. Add a possible complicated birth into the mix and it was the stuff of nightmares. Sophie catastrophised most situations anyway so this one was in danger of making her brain explode.

A sudden crack of thunder sliced through her silent reverie to startle her, making the soapy plate in her hand slide quickly back into the suds. The sky lit up, lightning flashing behind the dark clouds, and her heart beat a little faster. She was not a fan of storms. Where some people were content to watch the drama unfold and marvel at the power of Mother Nature, Sophie could be found blocking plugholes, turning off electrical devices and unplugging everything in case lightning struck the house. Even a one in a million chance was enough for her to take precautions.

Goodness knew how Molly was sleeping through all of this, but she needed the rest. To her credit she had taken the news about Jack's delayed return better than expected. Sophie supposed the couple were used to their lives being dictated by the weather, living on this remote island. She, on the other hand, had her days carefully mapped out and preferred to stick to her schedule. Despite the circumstances being beyond her control, it did not sit well with her having to phone and rearrange her other appointments. She didn't like going into the unknown unprepared.

Another boom of thunder reverberated, closely followed by a flash of lightning illuminating the gloom. Sophie shuddered. If she had been at home she would be tucked up in bed with the curtains closed and the covers over her head so she couldn't see or hear what was going on outside.

The next rumble seemed closer, louder than the last. She could still hear it when the world outside lit up again. Then Sophie realised the noise was coming from upstairs. Molly.

She placed the last dish into the rack, leaving the soapy water to drain away, and went to dry her hands.

'I'm coming. Hold on, Molly.' A tall order, she knew, if the baby was determined to make an early entrance after all.

By the time she got upstairs Molly was standing at the window, doubled over in pain. The sight was sufficient to snap Sophie back into her professional frame of mind. Labour and babies she knew how to deal with. Even when there were a few curve balls thrown in along the way.

'Hold my hand and just breathe through the pain.'

'That's easier said than done,' Molly managed to pant out through gritted teeth, grabbing hold of Sophie at the same time.

'Is this your first contraction?'

Molly nodded.

'Okay. It should subside soon and we'll try and get you into bed before the next one comes.' Sophie coached her breathing until the contraction subsided, her hand squeezed so tight she thought her circulation had been cut off at one point.

As soon as Molly was able to move again she helped her back into bed.

'It's too early. I need Jack here.' For the first time since Sophie had arrived Molly had fear in her eyes. No matter what happened, it was her job to keep her patient calm and reassured that everything was going to be all right. Regardless if she was having a wobble in confidence herself. Out here Sophie only had the contents of her medical bag to handle an emergency. There was not

nearly enough equipment to cover all even-
tualities.

'He'll be here as soon as he can. In the
meantime you've got me and I'm going to
make sure you and the baby have the best
care I can give you. Now, let's take a look
and see how things are progressing.' It would
be best for all concerned if Molly was simply
experiencing Braxton Hicks contractions,
practice for the real thing. The baby would
have a better chance all round if Molly made
it past the thirty-six-week mark.

Unfortunately, it soon became apparent
that this was the real deal. 'Okay, Molly,
you're four centimetres dilated. There's still
a long way to go, but I would prefer to get
you to a hospital as a precautionary measure
since this is technically an early labour and
because baby is facing the wrong way.'

The tears Molly had been so bravely trying to keep at bay now fell unchecked. She
was afraid and, if Sophie was honest, she
was too. They were so far out from the mainland that if there were any complications…
Well, it didn't bear thinking about.

'But how? If there's a storm coming no
one can get to us without risking their own
lives.' Molly was scrambling to sit up again
as panic took over, but Sophie needed her to

remain calm if they were to have any hope of slowing this labour down.

'I'll put in a call for the emergency helicopter. I'm sure they can still get to us, and they'll have more equipment on board to monitor you and the baby until we can get you to the hospital.'

Flying in a helicopter in a storm wasn't something she would ever have contemplated if it weren't for the benefit of her patient. Her parents would be proud. It was the sort of thing they would have done without a second thought for their safety. Certainly not for the young daughter they had left behind. Thankfully she had learned from her parents' mistakes. If she had to get on that helicopter it would only be because it was a matter of her patient's survival.

'That's it, Molly. You're doing so well.' Sophie wrung out the wet flannel into the basin on the night stand and placed it across Molly's forehead.

'I want Jack,' she sobbed, understandably emotional as her labour progressed, undeterred by the less than desirable circumstances.

'I know, sweetheart. I'm sure you will see him soon. For now we have to concentrate on getting you through these contractions.' Labour had progressed quickly, and she was already six centimetres dilated. This baby was coming tonight, with or without outside assistance. For everyone's sake, Sophie hoped she would not have to deliver this baby alone. It was not that she couldn't do it, goodness knew she had delivered babies in all sorts of situations. Her training and experience had prepared her well, but with a premature birth there were more risks involved and she didn't want to leave anything to chance.

'This isn't how it was supposed to be,' Molly groaned as another contraction took hold.

'I know it's not the home birth you'd quite expected, but what a story you'll have to tell. Choppered off the island to reunite with your husband is romantic in its own way.' As long as the baby didn't arrive before the helicopter and there were no life-threatening complications for mother or baby.

'Does Jack know the baby's coming?'

'The line wasn't great when I spoke to him again, but he knows and he's going to meet us at the hospital.' Only trouble being that she didn't know how long the helicopter would take to get here, if at all.

* * *

Molly's cries echoed through the cottage and there was nothing Sophie could give her to help her through the contractions. Even if she had been in hospital, her labour had advanced so rapidly there wouldn't have been time to give her an epidural if she had wanted one. This was the worst part for her and her patients, both powerless until nature had taken its course.

'This will all be worth it when you have that little baby in your arms,' she said, brushing Molly's damp hair away from her face. The stress, the pain and the whole labour often faded in the face of a brand-new life being brought into the world. For Sophie included.

Although she was still praying they would get to the hospital in time, it was looking more unlikely by the second with the closer contractions.

That didn't mean she wasn't relieved when she heard the noise of the helicopter over the house. Sophie couldn't leave Molly when she was in the last stages of her labour, but she did rush to open the bedroom curtains to see what was going on. It did nothing to allay her fears. The chopper was battling against the wind, struggling to land. A line was thrown out, it too swinging from side to side. A figure in bright orange risked life and limb to traverse it and Sophie's heart was in her mouth simply watching. At this stage she knew she was delivering this baby here and now and backup should have been a comfort. Instead, it gave her another life to fret over. In the end she turned away, unable to stomach witnessing the dangerous mission unfold.

It was only when she heard banging at the front door she was able to breathe again.

'The door's open. We're up here,' she shouted above the noise of the helicopter being buffeted about by the storm outside.

Whichever daredevil had been dispatched to assist her would have to do without a welcoming party as Molly panted frantically through her contractions.

'Okay. So where are we?' The heaven-sent paramedic had entered the room, but Sophie's relief was short-lived as she recognised the face as well as the voice. Roman Callahan, the man who had broken her heart and who all other men had failed to live up to since.

He was still as handsome as ever, his black hair tousled in that sexy devil-may-care way and with a lean, muscular body to remind her he was not a teenage boy any more. Sophie made the decision not to introduce herself. If he didn't recognise her she certainly wasn't going to remind him who she was and how they had parted over a decade ago. Although after being best friends for years it would be surprising if he didn't know her. That led her to conclude he was either trying to save her blushes or pretending not to know her to avoid rehashing the past. It was possible he also believed this birth was more important than their ancient history.

The last time she'd seen him was when they were eighteen, just before they'd gone their separate ways to university and she had made the impulsive decision to kiss him. That one rash decision to act on her teenage crush had ensured her best friend had walked out of her life ten years ago, never to be seen or heard from again. Until now.

Despite all the questions whirling around her mind about where he had been, what he had been doing and if he had ever thought about her, Sophie had to set her personal crisis aside to focus her attention on her patient. Since he hadn't chosen to acknowledge her in any other way than a professional capacity, she chose to do the same. For now. When this was all over she might have one or two things to say to him. All that was required of her now where Roman Callahan was concerned was to ignore her fast beating heart reacting to seeing him again. If she had a spare moment she would be completely humiliated to see him again.

'Ten centimetres dilated and the baby's head is crowning,' she told him after checking on Molly's progress.

'It looks as though you've managed on your own just fine, Soph. I don't think you needed me at all.' So he had recognised her after all. Even if it hadn't led to the tearful reunion she'd often dreamed about when she'd thought of running in to him again.

'Well, you're here now and Molly and the baby will still have to get to hospital.' Out of the corner of her eye she saw the flash of neon orange as her new colleague moved closer to the bed.

'Hello, Molly. I'm Roman and I will be your paramedic escort for the evening.' Apparently he was still the same flirt, the same joker he had always been. It might be reassuring for his patients, but not for an ex-friend who had spent the last ten years trying to get over him.

'Roman, could you get me some of those towels from the dresser?' If nothing else, he could make himself useful.

'Sure. I'm here at your disposal.' To his credit, he didn't immediately attempt to take over the situation, despite her call for help. He appeared to respect her position and experience as a midwife even if she had lost his friendship so long ago.

'When the next contraction comes, Molly, I need you to bear down and push this little one out. Okay?' It shouldn't be long now, and Sophie was reassured there was a chance of getting them to the hospital.

'You're doing really well.' Although Roman was looking at Molly as he passed over the towels, Sophie had a feeling he was talking to her. Perhaps it was her subconscious seeking reassurance but sometimes even a trained professional needed a confidence boost.

She spread a towel under Molly and could tell immediately when her body tensed up that the time had come. Whilst she got ready to catch the baby, Roman moved to the head of the bed.

'Time to push, Molly. I'm here and Roman's here and we are going to help you both through this.'

'Take my hand, swear at me, whatever it takes.' He took Molly's hand as she pushed through the contraction and Sophie watched Mother Nature take over, a new life slipping into her hands.

He was smaller than expected and Sophie moved quickly to cut and clamp the umbilical cord. She swaddled him in another of the towels and moved into the light where she could see him better.

'I want to hold my baby,' Molly cried, and Sophie had to ignore the swell of nausea in her stomach as she looked at the pale bundle in her arms. The baby still hadn't made a sound and had some staining on his skin, indicating that meconium was present. Sometimes baby could have a bowel movement and excrete the sticky green substance into the amniotic fluid. If inhaled, causing meconium aspiration syndrome, it could lead to severe lung problems.

She began rubbing his back, praying with every breath in her body that they would soon hear his cries.

'We just need to do some observation on the baby before you can hold him.' Roman was doing his best to placate Molly but it would soon become apparent all was not well.

'Come on, little one,' Sophie urged quietly, hoping she could somehow bring him back to life.

She felt Roman's presence beside her as she reached into the infant's mouth to clear anything which might be preventing him from breathing. They exchanged a concerned glance, sharing that overwhelming desire for a miracle. There was some meconium in the baby's mouth blocking his airway. Sophie took an aspirator from her bag and suctioned out the substance she could see.

'Do you want me to try?' Roman asked softly.

She was on the verge of agreeing and letting him take control, in the hope he could do what she could not, when there was a small ragged cry from the babe in her arms.

Their collective exhaled breath and the urge to weep signalled the relief that this might have a happy ending after all. When she looked into Roman's all too familiar eyes she could tell he was as moved as she by the moment.

'I think that's his way of saying he has had enough fussing,' she said, pulling herself together.

'I'll get him some oxygen to help with

his breathing.' Roman turned away to get the mask and pump from his bag, but Sophie didn't miss the swipe of his hand across his eyes. It was typical of him to resist expressing his emotions. That at least hadn't changed. He had always been difficult to read. She blamed him for letting her make a fool of herself, believing he loved her as much as she did him. Only to find out too late it had all been one-sided.

'Is everything all right?' Molly enquired.

'Roman's just going to give the baby some oxygen to help him breathe. He had some fluid in his airway, but I've cleared it. The hospital will do some X-rays to make sure there's nothing left in his lungs and give him some antibiotics to prevent possible infection, but he looks fine.' Sophie handed the now very vocal tot to Roman so she could attend to Molly to deliver the placenta and make sure she was fine to transfer to the helicopter.

She cast a glance over at Roman, who looked unexpectedly confident and content cradling a baby in his arms. It did little to help control her emotions when she'd spent much of her teens imagining this moment. Only with Roman cooing over their own child.

* * *

Throughout all the drama Roman had kept in touch with the helicopter crew and it was a relief when his walkie-talkie crackled to life with news that they had managed to set down outside.

'That's us, folks. Time to get moving.' He was holding the baby in one arm whilst hoisting his medical bag onto his other shoulder.

'Will…er… I have to fly too?' She would do it if she had to but being in a tiny tin can being tossed around by a storm was not in keeping with her idea of playing it safe.

'Not this time, sweetheart. I'm afraid we just don't have room on board.' The term of endearment casually tossed into the air had no less effect on her now than it had when she'd been younger. As a teenager she would have done anything to have him call her that in anything other than his usual teasing manner. It was easy to see with hindsight how a lovestruck girl could have mistaken his friendship for something she really wanted.

'I'm sure you'll give Molly and the baby the best possible care in my absence,' she assured Molly, along with herself.

It was hard to hand over responsibility of one of her patients. He seemed a very competent paramedic, but she knew nothing about Roman Callahan any more. On the positive side, at least in the hospital they could give the baby any extra care he might need.

'I'll get Jack to bring you back as soon as the storm dies down.' Molly eased herself up from the bed and Sophie helped her get dressed to protect her from the elements. Ideally, she would have some time to rest and recover so quickly after the birth but, as any mother, she was willing to set aside her discomfort for the sake of her newborn.

'Don't worry about me. It'll be nice to have some time on my own here and I'll get in touch with Clem in the morning. There's plenty of cleaning-up to do. I'll be fine.' The lie would be worth it to prevent Molly from fretting any further.

She thought she caught a flicker of something in Roman's eyes challenging her. It was possible he remembered her fear of the dark. A minor inconvenience in comparison to the things people like Roman, who put their lives on the line every day, did in the line of duty. At her age she really ought to have got over her childhood hang-ups, but that meant facing them head-on and she was the queen of procrastination when it came to dealing with her emotional baggage. To-night, on her own on an island in a storm was going to be a real test of strength for her.

They transferred their patients into the waiting helicopter, ducking below the ro-tating blades. Once she was satisfied Molly and her son were secured by the crew, So-phie stepped back. Her hair whipped about her face when the helicopter began to lift up off the ground. It was already getting dark but the lights from the chopper lit up ev-erything on the ground below as it took off, catching her in its spotlight.

Perhaps that was what prompted Roman to lean out for one last goodbye.

'It was good to see you again, Sophie,' he said, before the world around her was sud-denly plunged back into darkness. Leaving her all alone for the second time in her life.

CHAPTER TWO

ROMAN COULDN'T GET Sophie out of his head. Of course he had known he would probably run into her again after moving back to the area. It was possible that had prompted his decision to return in the first place. After every breakup, amicable or otherwise, it always made him think about Sophie and how she was doing. If she was happily settled down with someone else or what could have happened between them if he'd stayed and let something develop between them. Without doubt, his relationship with his parents would have been strained if not non-existent, as it was today.

When it came to Sophie though, there were still unresolved issues. His last partner, Lena, had asked him why he was so afraid to commit, and Sophie had been the first thing which came to mind, his thoughts turning to how he hadn't been able to give himself to her when she was the only person he had really loved, so how could he possibly settle for anyone else?

It had been pointed out to him in the midst of the breakup that he wasn't getting any younger and he would end up a sad, lonely man. The words had haunted him because it was probably true. He didn't want a wife and kids now, but what if he realised too late that he did but he was too set in his ways to share his life with someone else?

When the temporary position had come up in his home town he had believed it was the chance for him to get some closure. He knew he would run into Sophie at some stage and be confronted by his past but apparently he hadn't been prepared for the impact that would have upon him. Or was that the reason he hadn't actively sought her out? Deep down, had he known that seeing her again would make him question why he had left her in the first place?

They hadn't parted on the best of terms. One kiss between them had changed their relationship, and brought everything into sharp focus for him. He'd known he was in love with her, but a romance would never have worked between them. They were too different, and he knew he could never bring her the happiness she deserved. She was someone who needed stability and security, where he couldn't wait to break free from the shackles his parents had imposed upon him.

He didn't regret the decision to leave, especially when he'd seen first-hand how capable and confident she was in her job. In leaving his old life behind, he'd had the opportunity to experience much more than he ever would have staying in one place. He was always moving around, taking temporary placements where he could so life never got boring.

Sophie had never needed him, but he did miss her friendship. She was the only one he had ever been able to confide in, who'd understood him when his family never had.

He had left soon after their ill-fated kiss, going to medical school against his parents' wishes. Now he was back, and in some ways it felt as though he had never left.

Sophie was the same natural beauty she had always been. Her wavy dark brown hair was longer, her curves more pronounced, and now she had a confidence she had lacked in her adolescence. In short, she was breathtaking.

Roman was glad she had emerged from

the dark shadow of her parents' death. She had always seemed to judge herself by their standards and zest for life, believing she was in some way lacking for not being like them.

Though never in his eyes. Their friendship had blossomed during her grief. He had noticed her retreat from the world and recognised that loneliness. Even though he had family at home, he'd never felt as though he belonged there when his parents had always wanted more from him than he was prepared to give. They had pushed him to join the family business in land and property management, but he'd had dreams of his own to go into medicine which were not in keeping with their ingrained traditions. His older brothers had fallen in line, rendering him the black sheep of the family.

As it was the end of his shift he wasn't likely to see Sophie today and catch up on her life since they had parted all those years ago.

'Hey, Roman. Good to see you.' Theo Turner, an obstetrician at the hospital, crossed the corridor to speak to him.

'You too.' Roman shook his hand, genuinely pleased to see him. They had been introduced during his first day on the job and instantly seemed to hit it off. Although they didn't hang out after work, their schedules often clashing, Theo had been nothing but kind and supportive, asking how he was doing any time they ran into each other. Everyone seemed to respect him, and he came across as a genuine, compassionate soul who cared a lot for his patients and colleagues. The sort of man Roman wished he'd had as a father, as a male role model, growing up. Instead of an overcritical, controlling figure who had cast a dark shadow over his entire life.

'Another rescue mission? You've had quite a few recently.'

'Yeah, I think it has a lot to do with the time of year and the weather. People are more prone to accidents or can find it difficult to access medical help in some of the more isolated areas around here.' In the summer, his colleagues told him, they dealt with more beach rescues with swimmers in difficulty or those stranded out walking on clifftops. The winter brought dangerous icy roads, inhibiting patients and emergency services alike.

'We would all be lost without you.' Theo clapped him on the back. He had that unique ability to make everyone feel at ease, and Roman particularly. As though he was part

of the team here. It was nice to be appreciated and have his work validated. He didn't
let praise go to his head, but it did always
serve to remind him he had taken the right
path after all.

'That's very kind of you, but we just do
the picking up and dropping off. As a matter
of fact, I've just transferred a new patient.'

'We both know your job entails a lot more
than being an air taxi. You've saved countless lives where we couldn't get access to patients in jeopardy. Case in point being Molly
Matthews and her baby. They're doing well
now, but goodness knows what would have
happened if you hadn't been able to get out
to the island.'

'Now, I can't take credit for that one. Sophie had everything in hand by the time we
got there. I'm sure she could have managed
until the storm was over.' Although he hadn't
stopped thinking about leaving her behind
on her own. She didn't fool him. Despite the
bravado, he knew she'd had no desire to set
foot on that helicopter or be left in the dark.
She might be all grown up, but he was sure
there was some of the Sophie he'd known
still in there. He had seen the fear in her eyes
when the helicopter had lifted off, leaving
her alone in the dark, but he also knew she

would never have accepted him staying behind to look after her rather than their patients. She was too professional and proud to do that.

'Sophie French—the midwife from Carey House? Yes, she's great. We work a lot with the midwives there.'

'You know her well, then?' This could be a way to satisfy his curiosity without venturing into old territory to do so. He had a feeling that once he did he would be opening up a can of worms.

Theo smirked. 'Ah, has our young midwife caught your eye? It's not surprising, I suppose, when you find a beautiful young woman who is also smart and good at her job. The whole package.' There was a wistful look in his eyes that knocked the wind out of Roman. He had no claim over Sophie. Not since he had abandoned her. Yet, even after all these years, his first reaction to the possibility of another man taking an interest in her was to be jealous, possessive even. Sophie would have found that ironic.

'Are the two of you…together?' The word almost choked him, and it was then he realised that Sophie was part of the reason he had returned. Even if he had not known it until this moment, he had never really got over her. Now it appeared he was too late to do anything about it.

Theo chuckled and gave him another hearty slap on the back. 'Goodness, no. I'm still smarting from my divorce. Don't worry, as far as I'm aware she's unattached.'

Although relieved to find his new friend wasn't involved with his first love, Roman didn't want to risk gossip around the hospital before he had a chance to reconnect with Sophie properly. He wasn't sure what he expected if he saw her again, but he was sure she wouldn't appreciate being the subject of false rumours involving him. Although she hadn't challenged him about the past, it was probably only because they'd had other things to deal with at the time. Without a patient in premature labour taking priority, she might not be so amenable towards him.

'It's nothing like that. We grew up together in Carey Cove. I haven't seen her since we left school and I was simply curious about what she's been up to since.' He played down their past relationship since there was nothing to tell. They had looked out for one another as kids, but he had realised in the nick of time that Sophie could do better than him. Before he admitted he had feelings for her too and potentially ruined her life and disappointed her, the way he had his family.

'I didn't know you were a local.' Theo shook his head, clearly bemused by the information.

It wasn't something Roman had purposely kept secret, but he hadn't been back long enough to be comfortable sharing personal details about his life.

'Carey Cove born and bred, but I flew the coop a long time ago.'

'And now you're back. Were you homesick?' Theo teased, not completely off the mark.

'Something like that.' Growing up, it hadn't been the eight-bedroom, four-bathroom mansion which had been his sanctuary. It had been Sophie. She'd been home to him and Roman was feeling decidedly nostalgic.

By getting closure on their past, he wondered if it might help him to settle down in the future.

'Are you sure you want to take this on all on your own today? It's your day off. Wouldn't you rather take some time out for yourself? You've had a rough couple of days.' Kiara, one of the newer members of staff, was peering at Sophie as though she were one of their pregnant ladies needing a little coddling.

Sophie dumped another box on top of the pile already taking up residence in the hallway of Carey House.

'That's exactly why I need to keep busy. Too much time on my own lately. Besides, it's Christmas and it's about time it looked like it around here.' She had survived her night on the island, physically at least. Mentally, it hadn't been so easy, and it wasn't merely her fear of the dark keeping her awake. The shadows of the past had spooked her too.

That blasted Roman Callahan, dropping into her life like some kind of superhero, had totally rocked her usually ordered world. It didn't help that he had disappeared equally as quickly, leaving her with more questions than ever. Like what would have happened if he had reciprocated her feelings and they had stayed together?

These past years she had played it safe, whilst it seemed Roman had continued to live on the wild side. Taking risks and living life to the full. Her parents would have loved him. She didn't think they could ever have been compatible as a couple, but she would never find out. Her overactive mind, however, didn't stop conjuring up images of them being together and what it might have been like sharing her life with him over these past years instead of being on her own for most of the time.

Sophie unboxed one of the many Christmas trees they decorated the building with and began to unfurl the rustling plastic branches. Even though everything was fake, designed to give the impression of real snow-dusted fir trees, there was a real scent of cinnamon and citrus emanating from the packaging.

Once she had put the layered Christmas tree together she found a scattering of real pine cones lying in the box. Lifting one to inhale the scent, it became apparent the smell had not been a result of her overactive imagination after all.

'I'd forgotten about those. I made them with the local kids at the Christmas Fayre last year. I got roped in by Marnie to represent Carey House with a craft stall,' she explained to Kiara, who was watching her with the hint of a smile on her lips.

'What?' she asked, wondering if she was covered in as much glitter and fake snow as the pine cones.

'You are very distracted today. Not your usual focused self.'

Sophie knew it was not an insult, her colleague would never intend to hurt her feelings, but the comment stung nonetheless. She hated anyone thinking she wasn't giving her job one hundred percent, even on her day off.

Deciding it was best to be honest about what was going on rather than have someone think the worst about her, Sophie sighed. 'A blast from the past literally dropped in on me and it has kind of thrown me.'

'Oh?' Kiara, who had been on her way out of the door, now took a seat on one of the sturdy boxes, ready to hear the full story. The novelty of Sophie sharing any personal info apparently drew a captive audience. Nothing out of the ordinary normally happened to her and she was happy that way.

Of course she'd had a boyfriend or two over the years but those relationships had occurred organically, developing between her and men she generally got to know through work. Delivery drivers, their postman, even a male receptionist from St Isolde's for a while. None of those relationships had raised an eyebrow from her colleagues and, if she was honest, they had not excited her much either. She had chosen men she deemed safe and reliable, who wouldn't go off her and hurt her, as Roman had. The problem with that being that they lacked the excitement and skipping pulse which he'd brought. Something which had not changed, judging by their most recent encounter.

'The paramedic who attended Molly Matthews's birth, Roman Callahan. We...er... grew up together.'

'Ooh! Childhood sweethearts? Tell me more.' Kiara rested her head dreamily on her hand, waiting to hear the next great love story. As someone who had recently fallen head over heels, she thought everyone must be walking around with those same heart-shaped eyes. Sophie, however, remained sceptical about ever finding 'the one'.

Once upon a time she had believed that was Roman, later to be proved tragically mistaken. Since then it had been more of a case of 'this one will do', without anyone ever really rocking her world again. Something she had sworn until recently she did not need. Now she was curious about what that would be like, even for a little while. A bit of excitement to shake up her staid life might put some pep in her step.

When she was young and naïve she'd

thought she could have it all—romance, a career and a family of her own. Experience had made her more jaded about that being possible. Sometimes her ideas had clashed with those of her partner, the last one expecting her to give up work if they were going to start a family, something she wasn't prepared to do for anyone. If she became a parent, yes, she would give it her all, but not at the expense of her career. Her own mother had done that, and she believed that was partly what had caused her restlessness. Not that she'd been the most attentive mum either, which might have been born of resentment when having Sophie had changed her life.

Sophie did not want the same for her or any future children.

'Not really. Certainly not on his part, at least. I haven't seen him in over ten years and the unexpected reunion brought up a lot of old memories.'

'Roman Callahan… I think he's the guy who played Father Christmas. You know, the one who abseiled down from the helicopter at the fair?'

'That doesn't surprise me,' Sophie muttered. The sight of someone dressed in a fat suit and bushy white beard risking his life to deliver some presents had caused her to look away at the time, afraid one wrong move would end in tragedy and trauma for all those watching. It made sense that daredevil was Roman. Someone who had never prioritised his personal safety over a thrill.

'No offence, but I wouldn't have thought he was your type. He's so daring and charismatic I can see the attraction though.'

'Roman Callahan is the reason I don't take risks when it comes to dating.' That wasn't strictly true. Her parents had a lot to do with that too. After all, they had repeatedly abandoned her long before Roman, in favour of seeking thrills. Until they had left her for ever. With Roman going off to uni, it had simply compounded the idea that playing it safe was the only way to protect the broken fragments left of her heart. Now he was back she was not sure how to react. The fact that he had been home for a while and had not made any attempt to contact her said he hadn't missed her. Yet that didn't prevent her from constantly thinking about him and the one kiss they had shared.

Kiara stood up and brushed the dust and fake snow from her uniform. 'Maybe you should start. You certainly haven't been happy playing things safe. If I see him I'll put in a good word for you.'

'Don't bother—' Sophie began to say, but Kiara simply winked and hurried away down the front steps, leaving her to wonder if she had heard her or chosen to ignore her instruction. Either way, the prospect of seeing Roman again caused a tingle of anticipation to ripple along Sophie's spine. Her feelings hadn't disappeared just because he had.

Carey Cove hadn't changed much in the years since Roman had left. Walking through it was akin to time travelling back to his childhood, each building bringing long-forgotten memories flooding back into his mind. That was part of the reason he had yet to venture near his family home. Apart from delaying another inevitable confrontation about his life choices, he couldn't face the ghost of past arguments once he set foot on the property.

So he found himself heading towards the beach, which he associated with happier times. With Sophie. Thinking of her yet again, it made sense that when Carey House came into view, overlooking the rest of the main village, he should instead decide to veer up that way to make sure she was all right after the events on the island. They had literally stranded her there and though she projected that tough exterior, he knew better than most how easily it could shatter.

He had never paid much attention to the old stone building when he was younger, but now he could see it for the wonder it was in an area where the population had grown and needed extra medical facilities. The house had been converted into a hospital in 1900 to provide maternity services for the more rural areas and now, with expansion, provided GP access to the local community. There was even a field out the back for the helicopter to land, should they ever need it for emergencies.

'Hi. I was hoping to speak to one of the midwives today. Sophie French?' As he approached, a woman was leaving the building with her medical bag in hand.

'Are you one of our expectant fathers?'

'No, I…er…work with the air ambulance service. I wanted to make sure she was all right after the recent drama on the island. Roman Callahan.' He held out his hand and gave her his best disarming smile in the hope she would trust him enough to divulge Sophie's address.

It was rare for him to have time off and

rarer still that he should spend it in Carey Cove. If he didn't follow this up now there was the possibility their paths might never cross again, and that was suddenly an unimaginable thought.

The midwife's frown faded as she shook his hand. 'Nya.'

'Ah, Theo over at the hospital mentioned you the other day. He said to give you his best wishes if I should run into you.' Unfortunately the message only served to make her frown again, indicating that there was a history between them too.

'How is Theo? He hasn't come to Carey Cove for quite a while.'

Although Roman was not privy to Theo's private life, it certainly seemed that during their recent interactions he did appear more downbeat than usual. Perhaps it had something to do with his divorce, or not seeing his children as much as he would like.

'He always appears to be working any time I've been at the hospital. I'm not sure he's had much time off at all recently.' The news, though it explained Theo's absence, did nothing to placate Nya's concern. She merely nodded.

'Could you tell me where I could find Sophie? I'm not sure when I'll get over this way again. No rest for the wicked, eh?' Another smile and attempt to convince her he was not a stalker who couldn't be trusted with the knowledge of her colleague's whereabouts.

'She's probably at home, Christmas-ifying her house after going to town here.' Nya raised an eyebrow at the red and silver tinsel wrapped around the hand rail outside. It was then he noticed Sophie's signature decorate-everything-in-sight-with-twinkling lights-and-sparkle design. She loved to go over the top at Christmas. He figured it was her way of compensating for the family Christmases she never got to have.

His house had never been a bundle of laughs on the big day either. Although his parents had always spent a fortune on big, extravagant gifts, it was never on things he had wanted or had any interest in.

He and Sophie had enjoyed their own Christmas of sorts. Meeting up at some point, stealing away from their fake happiness to exchange silly handmade gifts that had meant more to him than anything his parents had ever splurged on.

'I don't know the address, sorry.' He should have kept in touch but after the way they had parted he had thought it best. By severing all contact he would not be tempted to do something stupid, such as kissing her again, or worse.

Now that they had reconnected he was sorry he no longer knew anything about her. For all he knew, she could have married, had children and a life which had nothing to do with him. In hindsight, it might not be a good idea to turn up unannounced. As usual he had been thinking only of himself and what he wanted.

Roman was ready to concede it was not meant to be and walk away when Nya stopped him.

'She's still at her grandmother's place. Sophie inherited the cottage when she passed away a few years ago.'

'Oh.' That one word couldn't possibly convey how hard those words had hit him. Sophie was all alone. She had lost the only family she'd had left and he had not been there for her. He knew how close she'd been to her grandmother, and he'd had a soft spot for the old lady too. She'd often brought him in and treated him as her surrogate grandson, fussing over him and making him feel wanted and welcome in their home.

In that moment Sophie's grief became his. That ache in the pit of his stomach told the tale of his loss and empathy for Sophie. Now he had to find her and apologise. He'd never meant to leave her here all alone.

'You didn't know?'

'No.'

The look on Nya's face at his admission said he couldn't possibly be a friend of Sophie's to have missed that traumatic event in her life. No one could have been sorrier than him about that.

'Perhaps I should phone and let her know you're coming…'

'Please don't. I want it to be a surprise,' he said, already making his way towards the cottage. He didn't want to give her the chance to avoid him when he had so much making up to do.

The scene as he crested the hill was as Christmassy as he could ever hope to set his eyes upon. Sophie, donned in a fluffy red jumper, was hanging fairy lights around the cottage door. All that was needed was a dusting of snow and perhaps a sprig of mistletoe to help break the ice. Without a medical emergency requiring their immediate attention, he couldn't predict how this meeting would go.

Roman was almost reluctant to interrupt her enthusiastic carol singing. She clearly hadn't heard him approach and he cleared his throat to alert her to his presence.

The singing abruptly ended as she spun around, pulling the string of fairy lights down around her. Leaving her trussed up like a Christmas tree.

'Sorry. I didn't mean to startle you.'

'You didn't,' she insisted, disentangling herself from the string of flashing lights.

He knew better than to argue with her when she was on the defensive. When she felt threatened, or on the back foot, she retreated into her spiky shell, fists figuratively raised and ready to fight. He shouldn't have expected anything less. Regardless of her happy, sequin-robin-embellished appearance.

'I wanted to see how you were. Nya told me where to find you.'

'I'm fine.' She turned back and began to reattach her decorations.

'Can I give you a hand with that?' He didn't wait for the inevitable 'no' or he would never get to say what he wanted.

With his extra height advantage he was able to hang the lights on the door lintel with ease.

'Thanks,' she muttered with noticeable reluctance.

At least with the sparkling garland hung, there was no reason for her to ignore him.

'I didn't know about your grandmother. I'm so sorry I wasn't here for you.'

She shrugged, pretending it was not the big deal he knew it to be, her eyes already brimming with liquid emotion. 'I wouldn't have expected you to come.'

Her dismissive tone at his genuine remorse was a blow. Not only because she didn't believe his sincerity, but because it highlighted the distance which had developed between them. The old Sophie would have cried in his arms and let him comfort her. He missed that emotional connection they had once shared. Something he had never come close to having with anyone else since.

In his daydream he had imagined by turning up here they would have a big heart-to-heart and she would forgive him, relieving him from his burden of guilt. It was asking a lot after the way he had left her. Which she had clearly not forgiven him for, but Roman wondered if she still thought of the kiss they had shared too. He had certainly never forgotten it. So much had happened in the interim and he wanted to explain why he had run out on her, but it wouldn't achieve anything. Telling her he'd thought he wasn't good enough for her wasn't going to change events. It could simply leave them both asking 'What if?'. Sure, they were bound to be different people after all this time apart, but something familiar remained between them that he wasn't ready to let go of again.

A fat drop of rain landed on his forehead, bringing him back to the present, followed by another and another. Sophie opened the front door. 'I suppose you had better come in.'

It wasn't the effusive invitation he wanted but he supposed she was right to be wary. Molly and the baby were fine, so he had no real pretext for being here other than their personal connection. No one could blame her if she was unwilling to cover old ground when it must have hurt her as much as it had him.

'Thanks.' He wiped his boots on the 'Merry Christmas' doormat before stepping into the cottage and he was immediately transported back to their schooldays. When he'd hung out here rather than going home to more arguments with his parents.

With the warmth of the fire in the front room, the smell of baking emanating from the kitchen and the quaint, old-fashioned décor, he half-expected Sophie's grandmother to pop her head around the door to say hello. It must have been tremendously difficult for her living here with the loss. They had been so close Roman envied their relationship, never experiencing that close bond with anyone in his family. By spending time here he had experienced that level of unconditional love second-hand at least.

'Why are you here, Roman?' She had politely brought him into the living room and invited him to take a seat, but he could tell by the defensive arm folding she didn't want him here.

'I was at the hospital and Theo said Molly and the baby are doing really well.'

'I know that. As her midwife it's my duty to know how she is keeping.'

'I also wanted to check in with you to see how you were after all the drama on Enys.'

'I'm fine. Clem picked me up in the boat the next morning.'

'Good. I'm sorry I didn't come to see you sooner, Sophie,' he blurted out his regret, which was even greater now with her giving him the cold shoulder.

'There's no need. We were both doing our jobs. I'm quite capable of surviving alone for one night. I've been doing it for years.'

'I'm not talking about just the other night.'

'I know. My answer still stands.' Sophie's unrelenting spikiness made Roman think he was fighting a losing battle in trying to make amends. They were very different people now and too much time had passed. He should have realised he couldn't simply walk back into her life and pick up their friendship again. That easy rapport they'd once had was gone, replaced by this awkward, uneasy tension.

'I should go...'

'Have you seen your parents yet?'

His decision to leave was postponed by the change in conversation. Not one he was particularly keen to pursue, but at least she was giving him some air time.

'I haven't been home. I'm renting a place close to the hospital. To be honest, I haven't spoken to my parents since I came back.'

'Don't you think you should? They might be miffed to find out you've been here all this time and haven't bothered to get in touch.' Sophie thawed enough to sit down instead of hovering, waiting for him to leave. Roman wondered if her concern towards his mother and father related to her own emotions surrounding his return.

'It's more complicated than you know,

Soph. I've barely spoken to them since I left for university. Just dropping back into someone's life isn't easy, you know.'

She cocked an eyebrow.

'I don't know how they'll react any more than I knew how you'd feel about seeing me again.'

'It was a lot,' she admitted, though he had known by her expression at the point of recognition on the island. He had chosen not to enter into a dialogue about their past relationship during the emergency, not only because it wasn't the time or the place but also because he hadn't been prepared either. Not that he was readier today, despite walking here with the sole intention of seeing her.

'I should have come to see you before now. I didn't know if you would want to have anything to do with me again.' The thought of Sophie hating him and experiencing it first-hand had been too much to bear. It had been easier to keep thoughts of her at bay. The same way he had got through the rest of his life without her.

'If we're going to go there I think I'll need a drink. I have some mulled wine on the stove if you'd like some?'

Roman was glad of the offer to fortify

himself. He had an inkling that the honest conversation they needed to have was going to be a tough one.

CHAPTER THREE

'IT SMELLS DELICIOUS.' Roman had followed Sophie into the kitchen and as she stirred the saucepan the heady smell of cloves, cinnamon and orange was already intoxicating.

Hearing his uncertainty about coming to see her lessened Sophie's ire towards him. He had thought about her at least and not simply swaggered in, expecting to pick up where they had left off, feigning ignorance over the hurt he had caused her.

It had caught her off-guard and with her defences lowered there was a chance those old feelings she harboured for him would come rushing back. Especially when he seemed keen to make amends by seeking her out in this manner.

'You can't have Christmas without mulled wine.' And memories, she added silently. Her gran had always made the drink specially at this time of year. Non-alcoholic, of course, but Sophie made a more adult version these days. A real winter warmer from the inside out.

She poured the hot liquid carefully into two glasses and handed one to Roman.

'Cheers.' She clinked her glass to his and took a hearty sip of the spiced goodness.

'Mmm… Just how I remember it. Although I think yours has more of a kick to it.' He smacked his lips in appreciation.

'We're both over eighteen so I think we're allowed to have a little tipple now.'

'I don't suppose you have any shortbread to go with it?' Roman grinned.

Gran had always made a tray of shortbread to serve with her mulled wine, and he hadn't forgotten. Sophie was glad she still stuck to family tradition, even though she usually had to bring it in to Carey House so she didn't eat it all herself.

She reached for the old biscuit tin on top of the fridge and pulled off the lid to reveal the sweet treats within.

Roman looked at her imploringly with his big brown eyes and she was thankful it was the only thing he was asking from her. One glance into those peepers and she'd be hypnotised into doing anything he wanted.

'Go on, help yourself.' To the biscuits

only. Everything else would have to be negotiated. If he was even interested. After all, he hadn't gone out of his way to contact her in all these years.

Roman selected a sugar-dusted star-shaped piece of shortbread and bit into it. He closed his eyes and sighed in ecstasy. That was when Sophie knew she was in real trouble, her body quivering with that same giddy excitement that used to overtake her when they were together as teenagers. All that past hurt, the years apart, dissipated as her body reawakened to the sights and sounds of her old crush.

'Just like Gran used to make.' He opened his eyes and smiled, which didn't help her to keep hating him.

'Years of practice. She wasn't able to make them for quite some time because of the arthritis in her hands in her later years, so I took over.'

'That's too bad. I'm sorry. She was a wonderful woman. I remember the two of us scoffing a whole tin of shortbread between us when she wasn't looking.'

'I think that was your idea and you ate most of it,' Sophie reminded him.

'We both got a scolding from your gran, but she never told my parents. I had a soft spot for her and, if I'm honest, I was envious of the bond you two had.' Roman finished his biscuit in two bites, his appetite as hearty as ever.

'I think she saw you as another waif and stray to look after.' Her gran had enough love to go around for everyone. Sophie didn't know why her mum hadn't inherited the same warm maternal instinct, but she was lucky enough to have had at least one nurturing relative growing up.

'I was grateful to have somewhere to come to, where I was welcome. I had a closer relationship with you and your gran than I had with my own family. We didn't spend a lot of time together. It only led to arguments.'

Back then Sophie hadn't given much thought to Roman being at her house all the time, glad to just have a friend for company. Looking back, she had never had the pleasure of staying at the big house on the edge of town where most people would have been content to live.

She had clearly been mistaken in her later years, when she had believed she was the attraction, but now she was more curious than ever. 'I would have thought your house had more to offer than this cottage.'

The same reasoning could be applied now.

All she could give him was wine and short-bread, when he had a whole lifetime to catch up on with his parents.

'I had a complicated relationship with my family. I was more comfortable here with you.'

'You make me sound like some ratty old security blanket,' she complained. 'Comfortable' was worse than 'nice'. It implied she was as exciting as a worn-out pair of slippers.

'Trust me, you were everything I needed.' The words, the sincerity and the intensity with which he was looking at her sent shivers dancing across her skin. If only it were true. Her mind took her by the hand and led her back to that scene when she had kissed him and he had rejected her, to remind her not to get carried away. The consequences were far too painful to make that mistake a second time.

'Whatever happened between you and your parents, I'm sure you can work it out. Perhaps this is the time to check in with them.' It would focus his interest on something other than her, and give her some breathing space.

'Do you know how they are? Have you seen them?'

'Sorry, I don't know them very well and I don't think they mix in the village that much.'

'That would be right. They probably order everything in from London rather than mingle with the great unwashed.' Despite Roman's eye-rolling, Sophie didn't believe him to be joking about their snobbery. It would explain how she didn't know them even after growing up in the same village.

'At least you still have family.' Only someone who had lost everyone close to them could see how utterly futile in-fighting was in a family. It was a waste of precious time together and it made her blood boil when she didn't have that chance. She would have given anything to have one more day with hers. Even her parents, who she had never bonded properly with the way she had with her gran. She didn't think there was anything that couldn't be resolved with time and the reminder that you only got to have one family.

'I didn't mean to be insensitive. Sorry, Soph. It's just that my happiest memories are of being with you here.'

'Yeah. Gran knew how to make everyone feel safe and loved.' She hadn't understood how important that had been to Roman as much as her until today.

'I'm not talking about your gran, Sophie. I don't know what I would have done without you back then.'

Sophie's skin prickled as Roman set his glass down and moved closer. A sense of panic gripped her, knowing she was already lost to him again. If he wanted to renew their acquaintance, she knew she would jump at the chance. Regardless of the risks.

'You could have fooled me. From what I recall, you couldn't wait to get away from me.' She tossed back the rest of the wine, letting it burn her throat, bringing the pain of the memory to life.

They had been celebrating the end of their high school days, partying at a schoolmate's house with the rest of their year. Whilst everyone had been getting drunk and pairing off, they had spent the night cosied up discussing their future plans. They were going to spend the summer together before university and had talked about going travelling. It had given Sophie hope that there was more than unrequited love between them.

Over the years she had watched Roman flirt with and date every other girl he came across, all the while yearning for him to see her in the same light. She had dated but no one made her feel the way Roman did. From the time he had reached out to her when her parents had died, she'd harboured a crush which only got stronger the more time they spent together. He'd been different with her than he was in school, where he was a Jack-the-Lad daredevil. She got to be with the more caring Roman, who had always been there as a shoulder to cry on.

The fact that he had chosen to sit with her rather than show off at the party, the way he usually did, gave her reason to believe he had some feelings for her. She even believed they were having a moment when they stopped talking and he was looking at her the way she had longed for him to do for so long. That was the only reason she had moved in for the kiss. If one of them hadn't made the move, she thought she was going to be friend-zoned for ever and with them planning on going to different universities Sophie was afraid she would lose him if she didn't show him how she felt.

She'd lost him anyway.

'I wasn't rejecting you, Sophie, but my life here. I needed to start over and at that point in time I thought you did too.'

It was a twist on everything she had ever

believed about the situation. Not once had she considered that Roman hadn't kissed her back because he was thinking about her future. Suddenly it opened her mind to what could have been and everything they had possibly missed out on together. It was one thing if it had been a mutual attraction Roman had decided not to follow up. Quite another if the pain resulting from their lack of communication had dictated the safe, boring nature of her subsequent relationships. That need to protect her heart had controlled her love life and now she was discovering it had all been for nothing. Sophie was feeling very hard done by, to say the least.

'We were friends, Roman. You didn't even try to contact me. Do you know how much that devastated me?' Not only had she lost her best friend of eight years, her constant companion through grief and school and all other teen dramas, but she had lost the love of her life. He'd cast her aside so easily it had been a brutal blow to her poor fragile heart.

Roman sighed and at least hung his head in shame when reminded about his behaviour. 'I did think about it, Soph, believe me. I had feelings for you, but it wouldn't have been fair to either of us to act on them.'

'You…you had feelings for me?' The

knowledge that it hadn't been a one-sided affair after all justified her actions that night and she could at least stop blaming herself for driving him away. However, his admission still left a lot of unanswered questions. The most pressing one being why he hadn't returned her kiss that night.

'Of course I did. I wouldn't have spent all my time with you if I hadn't thought so much of you. I was afraid of ruining everything between us by making a move. You know I didn't stay with a girl very long before moving on to the next.' He smirked at that but Sophie wasn't finding anything amusing about the situation. By keeping her in the dark all this time he had made her doubt herself and everyone else who subsequently came into her life.

'You never thought about how much it hurt me to see you with a string of other girls?' He must have known how she'd thought of him by then and his colourful dating history seemed to be rubbing her nose in the fact she couldn't hold his attention. It had made her feel as though she wasn't pretty or interesting enough for him to be with on a romantic level. It had crushed her self-confidence as well as her heart.

'I'm sorry, Soph. I don't know what to

say, other than I was a teenage boy who didn't know how to deal with his emotions. I thought I could ignore them but then things came to a head that night…'

'Why…how could you reject me like that, Roman?' She was dismayed by the tell-tale hitch in her voice as she regressed to that spurned girl, so lost and alone when he had walked away.

Roman got up out of his seat and walked over to her, the close proximity and the intensity of his gaze upon her making Sophie shift uncomfortably in her chair when she was vulnerable and exposed.

He took her hands in his as he sat on the settee beside her. 'I never meant to cause you pain, Soph. Believe it or not, I thought I was doing the opposite and saving you from getting hurt. I loved you, I wanted you, but I couldn't see us together.'

'I wish you had told me that,' she muttered, wanting to weep for that young girl who had been mortified when he had pushed her away and left the next day without as much as a goodbye. If he had only explained his motives and told her he was leaving, it might have relieved some of the sorrow.

'What good would that have done? We never had a future together, both going in opposite directions with our lives. You would never leave Carey Cove, I knew that, and I was restless, desperate to get away. I didn't want to give either of us false hope.'

He had never given her a chance to explore the idea of moving away, but he was probably right. She had too many memories here—the only real connection to her family were the graves at the cemetery. This house, where she had lived with her grandmother for so long, was the one place she truly felt safe. She hadn't even redecorated so she could keep that feeling of familiarity and security, even without her beloved guardian's presence. Still, he should have at least attempted a conversation about his decision when it had directly impacted on her. If she had been given a say in what happened next her life could have turned out very differently. That loss of control, that sense of being abandoned was the same as when her parents had died and she had spent the intervening years avoiding that same hurt.

'I thought it was me. That I was the reason you left so suddenly, and I'd messed everything up because you didn't think of me the same way I thought of you.'

He tilted her chin up, forcing her to engage in eye contact and making her pulse skip. 'Hey, I was showing a lot of restraint, trust me.'

This time she knew she wasn't imagining the spark reigniting between them. Older and with more experience, Sophie knew the signs when a man was interested. Roman's darkening pupils and husky voice were strong indications that he saw her now as more than a childhood friend.

It was electrifying and her heart was beating so quickly with anticipation of what might happen she was afraid she might pass out and miss it.

Roman was everything her life was lacking—he was excitement and danger personified. They were too different to have any sort of future together, that certainly hadn't changed, but for a short while Roman might just be what she needed to shake things up around here.

'Don't you wonder what could have happened between us if we had acted on that kiss?' Now it was all she could think about. All those fevered fantasies she'd had about the two of them were now allowed to play out uninhibited in her head.

If they did give into temptation just once, now that they had cleared the air, it would give her closure on that part of her life. It would also validate her actions and feelings way back then, which was important to her when she had been blaming herself for so long for Roman leaving. Plus, it had been an age since she'd shared a bed with anyone, and she just knew he would absolutely rock her world.

She had been brave once, in showing him how she felt, and this time they were older and wiser, no longer two naïve kids who couldn't express themselves adequately. They were adults and she definitely wasn't the same Sophie who'd believed in happy-ever-afters. All she wanted tonight was validation that she was as good as any other girl Roman had been with.

'Of course I thought about it, but the timing was all wrong.' There was nothing he had wanted more than to take Sophie into his arms and his bed, but that was the one time he had decided to play it safe. She wasn't the kind of girl to sleep with on a whim. He had known it would have been a big decision for both of them and had been afraid it would change his mind about leaving.

That didn't mean he hadn't lain awake at night imagining what it would have been like.

'And now?' Sophie cocked her head to

one side, a slow smile spreading across her mouth. It was difficult to tell if she was teasing him or attempting to flirt. In which case she really was different from the shy Sophie he'd had to coax out of her shell when they were kids.

'What are you saying, Sophie?' It had been a while since he'd had any sort of relationship. He didn't tend to stick around in one place for too long. There was less chance of him disappointing anyone else that way. Although he had already done that with Sophie, so he had nothing to lose.

She reached up and popped open the top button of his shirt. 'I'm saying we could make up for lost time and opportunities.'

Roman could hear the blood pounding in his ears as she made a start on the second button. He grabbed her hand to halt her progress.

'That would be playing with fire, Sophie.' He couldn't promise her anything more now than he could then, and she still deserved more than him.

'I'm single and I presume you are too. Maybe we could both do with things heating up around here.'

Roman's heart rate was rising as rapidly as his libido. 'We might burn ourselves out.'

'It's a risk I'm willing to take.'

'Sophie, I'm only in town for a while. On a temporary placement. I can't make any commitment to you.' He didn't want to deceive her. If they were finally going to give in to those urges they'd apparently felt towards one another, he needed her to know it would be a one-time deal before he moved on.

'Perfect. I don't want one.'

Roman was mesmerised by Sophie's parted lips and the mischievous twinkle in her blue eyes. If this was her way of getting back at him for leaving her he was going to call her bluff. One hot and heavy kiss and she would realise how dangerous this idea could be. Sophie French would never be someone to willingly court danger. He, however, embraced it with open arms.

He placed the hand still held in his around his neck and pulled her closer to him. Roman intended the kiss to be punishing, his mouth hard on hers to make her see this would be a mistake. Except having Sophie in his arms was everything he wanted. No woman had ever matched up to her. He had never had the same connection or the shared history which had made them so good together.

Sophie had been his first love, his only

true love, and the one he had let slip away. Now she was kissing him back, giving him a second chance to undo that mistake, he couldn't remember why he was fighting against the idea.

She was moaning softly against him, draped sensually along his body, breaking through the pretence that this was nothing more than working through unresolved issues. Now it was about expressing his regret, how much he had missed her and how much she still turned him on.

That hard, unyielding lesson in doing the right thing was now a tender kiss full of yearning and passion. This time he was being honest about his feelings instead of hiding from them, instead of trying to convince Sophie they were different.

'You know where my bedroom is,' she whispered in between greedy kisses.

Heaven help him, she wasn't doing anything to help convince him this was wrong. Just like last time, it was going to be down to him to end things and keep Sophie protected. Except he wasn't sure that had been the right move after all. If it had been, then why were they right back here ten years later? Still wanting each other and no one else.

Perhaps if they had given in to those urges

that came with the first flush of young love, the shine would have eventually worn off. After being denied the pleasure of one another too long, that wanting had flared back to life with a vengeance.

'Sophie, is this really what you want? I can't promise you anything more than today.'

She took him by the hand and faced him with a determination he didn't ever remember seeing in her before. 'It's only sex, isn't it? Who says I want or need anything more than that?'

It was all the confirmation Roman needed to finally give in to that fantasy he'd had about her since they were teenagers. However, as he followed her to the bedroom he had a feeling they were both trying to fool themselves that this wasn't going to change things for ever.

Sophie's bravado was fuelled by lust alone. She knew if she didn't take this opportunity she would never take that walk on the wild side she had always dreamed about. With him only in town for a short time there was less chance of her getting her heart broken again. There wouldn't be time for her to fall for him all over again and invest in a future that was never going to happen.

Now she would find out if being with Roman was all hype conjured up in her mind over the years or if he was just like anyone else who had shared her bed. If that was the case there was no need to get her knickers in a twist over it. To her, sex had never been particularly mind-blowing and she would admit to being curious about whether it might be different with Roman.

The concept of what she was getting into made her legs tremble as she pushed open her bedroom door and led Roman inside.

'It's exactly how I remember it,' Roman commented with a smile.

Sophie never took much notice of her surroundings when they were so familiar to her. Looking at it through Roman's eyes made her cringe. It was the same frothy pink room they'd hung out in as teens. He would think she hadn't moved on at all from that naïve girl he had left on the beach a decade ago.

'If it ain't broke don't fix it…' She shrugged, wishing she had at least unpinned the photographs of her and Roman on her noticeboard. At least the *Mrs Sophie Callahan* and *Sophie + Roman = 4 ever* doodles had been consigned to the back of old school notebooks and were not in plain sight.

'No… I just thought…you didn't move into your gran's bedroom.'

It had never occurred to Sophie to take over the main bedroom. She might be the new owner and sole occupant of the house but in her head it would always be her gran's.

'It would seem disrespectful to take anyone in there.' What with all the sex she had not been having.

She swore she saw Roman flinch at the mention of other men, and it went a long way to restoring her confidence. Perhaps there was a tiny bit of him which thought of her as his.

'Now, where were we?' She popped open some more of his shirt buttons so they could refocus on what they'd been doing previously.

'I think you were telling me you only wanted me for my body.'

'Is that so difficult to believe?' Sophie yanked open his shirt, uncaring as the last couple of buttons pinged across the floor. She needed to convince him she was not a naïve spinster who couldn't handle the idea of a sex-only liaison. Only time would tell if that was true, but she wanted to try.

Peeling his shirt off, revealing the manly

chest nestled within was a feast for the eyes. The rounded biceps, the solid pecs and rippled abs were clearly the result of his physical adventures. Along with the light dusting of hair, his body was telling her he was no longer his scrawny teenage self either. He was all man, and she wasn't sure she knew what to do with him.

She'd had lovers but within the parameters of a safe relationship. A love by numbers playbook where there were no nasty surprises. Or excitement, if she was honest. This burning need inside for Roman was new to her. At least on this adult level.

It's just sex, she repeated in her head, reaching for the fly on his trousers and unzipping him.

'Hey, just because this is on a physical only basis, it doesn't mean we have to rush things.' Roman tilted her chin up so she was looking into his eyes instead of focusing on undressing him, making her melt all over again.

He bowed his head to capture her mouth, Sophie's eyes fluttering shut as he did so. The soft pressure of his lips took her back to that day when she had last thrown caution to the wind. Before everything was ruined.

This time they were literally going along for the ride.

The feel of Roman's hand sliding under her jumper was unexpected, but his warmth was a welcome salve against the goose-bumps on her skin. Sophie let him set the pace, happy to follow his lead. After all, he was the one known for taking risks and he had survived this far.

He stood back and whipped off her jumper before expertly unhooking her bra. Sophie gulped, a rush of arousal encompassing her body as he devoured her with his gaze. There was no doubt he wanted her, answering the one question which had plagued her all these years.

He came for her mouth again, this time the tender connection a passionate yearning she shared. While his lips and tongue were causing havoc upon hers, his hand was caressing her breast, his thumb teasing her nipple to attention. Making out like this was something they should have done as teenagers—the sort of after-school activity which could have got her into serious trouble. Second base only made her eager to hit that home run.

Roman left her gasping when his mouth fastened around her nipple, sucking and licking until she was fit to burst from sheer ecstasy. She could hear her heavy breathing, responding to Roman's groans of pleasure as he tasted her sensitive peaks of flesh. He was taking her to places she had only visited briefly before, and that had been on her own when her partner had failed to satisfy her. It was all she could do not to jump his bones like an eager to learn, born again virgin. Then she really would be showing her naivety when it came to the sort of sexy flings Roman was obviously used to.

He was kissing his way down her belly now, causing her to suck in a shaky breath as he came to the waistband of her reindeer-print leggings. With his hands on her hips, he slowly eased them down, dipping his tongue down further with every exposed inch of skin.

Her breath was coming in short, shallow bursts to match the frantic beat of her pulse. Could he feel what he was doing to her? She couldn't help but wonder if it was like this for him every time—exciting, breath-stealing... intoxicating. Indeed, was he even enjoying this as much as she was? When he pulled away her underwear and thrust his tongue into that most intimate place she could no longer think about his pleasure when she was completely focused on her own.

* * *

Roman buried his head between Sophie's thighs to taste the sweetness of her arousal. If this was the only chance they had to be together he wanted them both to remember it with a smile on their face. He took his time, savouring every moment of passion and each drop of Sophie's arousal. She came quickly, as though she had been waiting for him to touch her and trigger this release of teenage hormones he had fought so hard against.

He could see why. This was playing with fire. Sophie had insisted that she was not expecting more than one night but, as before, Roman couldn't be sure it would prove enough for him. He still wasn't the right person for her long-term, always moving around, never staying in one place too long, while Sophie was content living the life she always had. The fact she was even giving him a chance to redeem himself was a miracle in itself and that was what he intended to do. For one night he could make her happy and help them both move on from the past. Hopefully without losing his heart or mind in the process.

Sophie's panting breaths and quivering legs drew his attention back to the present. He feverishly kissed his way back up her body, doing his best to memorise every bit of her so he could finally stop wondering about what he had walked away from in the past. Although her magnificent naked body once seen would not be easily forgotten. He doubted the wanting would ever stop. All he could do was be thankful he had this time with her.

Sophie wrapped her arms around his neck as he kissed her heartily on the mouth. He grabbed her legs and hoisted her up around his waist to carry her over to the bed. She clung to him as he stripped away his own clothes, before tumbling onto the bed together. With the condom he had taken from his pocket he made sure they were safe from creating any unwanted complications before he joined their bodies together.

He had not been a virgin for a very long time, but it somehow felt like his first time when he slid into Sophie's wet warmth. Excited as a schoolboy, he couldn't get enough of her. Natural instinct took over, dictating the frantic pace. So much for taking things slowly, but they had waited a long time for this. Besides, Sophie was crying out for more with every hard thrust inside her, clearly enjoying losing control with him.

Sophie captured his face in her hands,

forcing him to look into her eyes and see the undisguised passion for him burning bright. He kissed her again, expressing that longing, his desire and admiration for her from the very depths of his soul.

When she tightened around him, her throaty cries becoming high-pitched, Roman knew she was close to orgasm again already. How quickly he was getting used to knowing her body. With time he was certain they could be phenomenal together, but the future was an option they didn't have. For the moment they had to simply revel in the ecstasy they were creating here and now.

Making love to Sophie was something he had only dreamed of, and it was fulfilling his every fantasy. She was so responsive and unexpectedly vocal it was an ego boost for the man who had let her down once too often.

He anchored one of her legs to his hip so he could plunge deeper inside, eliciting a sharp intake of breath from her.

'Are you okay?' He slowed down, not wanting to hurt her, regardless of the blood pounding in his head making him unable to think straight.

'Don't stop,' she gasped, biting playfully

at his neck and tearing through the remnants of his restraint.

He held onto the headboard of the bed for support and thrust; that sensation pulling him in deeper, tighter was something he could easily become addicted to.

Relentlessly chasing that ultimate release left him dizzy and Roman climaxed harder than he ever had before. Years of holding back from this exact moment. Utter bliss.

'Wow.' He had no other words to describe what had just happened, even if he had enough breath left in his lungs to speak.

'Uh-huh,' Sophie concurred, apparently suffering from the same affliction.

They took some time out, lying side by side staring at the ceiling until they recovered. Eventually Roman was able to speak again.

'Are you okay? Was that okay?' He was uncharacteristically concerned about his performance. Not that he didn't usually care about his partner but he was confident in bed. It was different with Sophie. Tonight could be their one and only time together. If she hadn't enjoyed it as much as he had she might come to regret it. It would also ruin the chance of a repeat performance, should the occasion present itself again. After what he'd experienced he wouldn't say no.

Sophie rolled over onto her side, pulling the mussed bed sheets up to cover her nakedness. She stared up at him, a wry grin crossing her kiss-swollen lips.

'More than okay. We must do this again some time.' Although she was teasing him, Roman was struggling not to get his hopes up.

Sophie held her smile in place, waiting for Roman's reaction. If he rejected the idea she could laugh it off as a joke. Regardless that inside she would crumble if he said no to her indecent proposal. He had unlocked a whole new world for her, shown her what she'd been missing, and she wanted to enjoy it a little longer. It would be cruel to make her inner sex goddess a prisoner again after her liberation.

Roman was not a safe option. He had already broken her heart once. However, he was definitely the best lover she had ever had to date. Perhaps it was because they knew each other so well, or it could be down to the fact that they were complete opposites. Whatever it was which caused the explosive chemistry between them, she wouldn't be human if she didn't want to test it again. And again.

If she could remember this time around that Roman wasn't the one, simply a fantastic time, there was no reason they couldn't have an adult fling with no expectations other than making each other feel good.

She'd managed to get Roman's attention.

'Sophie, as much as I would love to, I'm not looking for anything serious. You know that. I don't do long-term. With anyone.'

'If I wanted anything serious I wouldn't be here with you.' She was trying to be flippant when he had made it clear he didn't want anything requiring a commitment, but she saw him flinch. Apparently he had feelings to hurt, regardless of his cavalier attitude towards relationships.

Given his long-standing feud with his parents, it wasn't clear if Roman would even be staying long and she was counting on that to avoid falling for someone so unsuitable again. She could enjoy being with him while it lasted, armed with the knowledge it wouldn't be a long-term arrangement. Once he was gone she could return to her safe old life, no longer having to wonder about what could have been.

Sophie could enjoy that walk on the wild

side with Roman that she had been so fearful of and have the memories to last a lifetime. Hopefully minus any more scars.

Roman sat up. 'You would really be all right about keeping this a strictly sex thing?'

It was impossible to read his face but there was a flare of something in his eyes that suggested he might be excited by the prospect. She knew this was all he was offering and to read anything more into it would be foolish. Why shouldn't she have fun for once?

'I'm a grown woman, Roman, not a naïve teenage girl. I no longer believe in happy-ever-afters.'

'That's a shame. You deserve one.' He traced a finger along the curve of her shoulder, bringing goosebumps to the surface of her skin at the slight touch.

'I'll settle for a happy-for-now,' she insisted, dismissing the notion he should feel sorry for her. Until he had shown up again she'd been content with her lot, unaware that anything was missing from her life. Now she feared she would get too used to this post-sex bliss and confuse it with true happiness, something she wasn't convinced she had experienced, without another trauma stealing the moment from her. This time around she was calling the shots and attempting to get control of her emotions.

'So…this isn't a one-off?' He let his wandering hand slip down to the indent of her waist and the curve of her buttocks before drawing her possessively close. Inwardly, Sophie was squealing with delight but remained cool on the outside, as though this casual attitude was the norm for her.

'Not if you don't want it to be.'

'That sounds like an offer I don't want to refuse.' Roman rolled over on top of her, kissing his way along her neck and setting off fireworks throughout all of her erogenous zones.

To make this work they would have to set down ground rules, boundaries that would keep her heart from disintegrating when it came to an end.

At this moment all she cared about was prolonging this euphoria Roman was causing throughout her entire being.

CHAPTER FOUR

'HAVE YOU DONE something different with your hair today?' Nya Ademi, their head midwife, asked Sophie as she gathered her notes and bag to begin her rounds.

'No, I just wash and go, as always.'

'Hmm. Maybe it's your make-up. You've definitely got a glow going on,' Kiara offered, peering closely at her.

Heat suffused her cheeks at being studied so intently. 'I haven't done anything different. Now, if you don't mind, I have pregnant women to attend to.'

'Well, whatever you're doing, you're out-glowing every one of our mothers-to-be. You're not expecting, are you? We've got a temporary replacement starting at the beginning of December while Marnie's on maternity leave, but it'll be tough going if we lose you too.' Nya was teasing and even though they had taken precautions Sophie's hesitation to consider the possibility handed her colleagues all the ammunition they needed. It was the astonished gasps which prompted her into a response.

'I am not pregnant.'

'But you're seeing someone?' It was clear Kiara had kept the secret about Roman to herself, not sharing even with their superior. They were not a gossipy group and Sophie thanked her lucky stars she worked with such lovely people.

With anyone else this wouldn't have been headline news but because it was Sophie, someone who kept herself to herself and only dated people she got to know first, it was apparently the lead story. They crowded around her, waiting for the big reveal. Sophie knew they only wanted to be happy for her but she wasn't ready to share the details of the arrangement between her and Roman. In the cold light of day it might sound seedy.

It had been different lying naked in bed with him, agreeing to a casual fling. Continuing a strictly physical relationship was the most she could hope for with Roman. Not least because he would be moving on again. By his own admission he was only here as a stopgap. Goodness knew what had brought him back in the first place, it certainly wasn't his family, but Sophie was glad he was here even temporarily. In fact it was probably better for her, so she wouldn't have a chance to get too attached to him again. This was likely her one chance to be with Roman and she had grabbed it greedily with both hands. A short-lived fling with Roman was possibly the only way she would survive being with him, knowing from the outset that it wasn't for ever.

However, admitting that was all it was to her friends would make her sound sad and desperate for accepting those terms. In the end she decided to keep the details private.

'I am seeing someone but it's early days.'

'Aw, I'm glad you've met someone.'

'I'm so happy for you.' Kiara sounded relieved she could actually talk about it freely now.

The strong hugs and excited squeals which followed her news were heart-warming but also a tad disconcerting. She was touched that her friends were excited for her, but at the same time it said a lot about how boring her stale life had become to cause such hysteria with a romantic interest on the horizon.

'Thanks. It's nothing serious,' she reiterated.

'Anyone we know?'

'Er…' It was a tricky one. Sophie didn't want to lie but also didn't relish her fling with Roman being common knowledge, making it into something it wasn't—a relationship.

'Just one of the paramedics from St Isolde's.' It was partly true but if she had mentioned he was on the helicopter crew they would have known exactly who she was talking about. It wouldn't have taken people long to uncover their history and she and Roman were trying to put the past behind them.

'I hope everything works out for you, love.' Nya gave her another hug, satisfied with that small amount of information.

The others wished her well too before setting off for their working day.

Sophie was still smiling as she climbed into her car. Catching sight of herself in the mirror, she could understand why her colleagues had quizzed her. She was positively radiant. As though that warm satisfaction Roman had brought her had spread from the inside out.

Even thinking about their night together gave her the same sort of head rush she got when she stood up too quickly. Was this the same adrenaline buzz he got from all of his crazy adventures? In which case she could see why he was always seeking the next one. At least great sex wasn't as life-endangering as climbing mountains or dangling from helicopters if she became hooked on this feeling.

It was provident that she had work today or they might have worn each other out completely in bed. The lack of sleep wasn't something she could sustain long-term, even if their nocturnal activities had been oh-so-pleasurable.

This was her reality. Sleeping with Roman was merely a romantic fantasy which would probably be over all too soon, but she would enjoy it whilst she could. Before feelings and expectations barged in to ruin the illusion.

'Hi, Nina. How are you this morning?' Sophie wiped her feet on the doormat before entering her heavily pregnant patient's home.

'Exhausted. As you can see, I haven't even had time to get dressed this morning.' She pulled at her shapeless, food-encrusted nightdress.

'Rough night?' Sophie closed the door behind her and followed Nina into the kitchen, where her toddler was playing in a bowl of cereal in her highchair.

'This one was up half the night teething.

Not that I could sleep anyway when my heartburn was so bad.'

At this late stage of pregnancy it wasn't an uncommon complaint, with the baby pressing against most of the vital organs. It could be an uncomfortable time for a lot of Sophie's patients.

'Can your husband help you out a bit more at night?' With a toddler to take care of and a baby on the way, Nina was going to have to learn to delegate some of the responsibility elsewhere or she would burn herself out.

'Dean was working away from home last night. His last overnight shift before the baby arrives. He'll be back later to take over.' Nina leaned back, manoeuvring herself onto the sofa in the living room, not bothering to stop the little one from splashing any more milk onto the floor.

'That's good. I tell you what, I have some time before my next appointment. Why don't I look after little Amy and let you go have a soak in the bath?'

Nina's eyes lit up at the suggestion. 'Are you sure?'

'Of course. It will be better to take your blood pressure after you've had a nice relaxing bath.' For Sophie, part of her duty to her patients was looking after their mental health too. It wasn't the first time she had done a spot of babysitting to give one of her mums a well-deserved break. She didn't mind. With no other family, she had never had the chance to coo over babies at family gatherings and she did enjoy the opportunity when it arose.

She had always pictured herself settling down with a husband and family. Creating the scene she had never had for herself in Carey Cove. However, as time had gone on and her relationships had failed one after the other, she had begun to think that having a baby of her own was never going to happen. She didn't want to bring another child into the world without the love and stability of two parents. So far there hadn't been anyone in her life who saw themselves being with her for ever. Sophie was beginning to think she was completely unlovable, so Roman had come at just the right time to give her an ego boost. Even if it wouldn't have the final outcome she had always hoped was possible.

'I was about to wash and change her.' Nina pointed to the changing mat and basin of water sitting on the table.

'That's fine. I'm sure I can manage,' Sophie assured her with a smile. It was enough to get Nina back on her feet, the lines of tension across her forehead already evening out.

'Well, Miss Amy, it looks like it's just you and me.' Complete with sound-effects, Sophie aeroplaned the rest of the baby's breakfast into her mouth. Amy babbled contentedly as her new babysitter cleaned up the mess on her highchair tray and made no complaint when she was lifted out.

Sophie stripped off the milk-sodden sleepsuit and nappy to wash her all over with a flannel. She couldn't get enough of those baby giggles when she tickled her tummy or the little hands grasping for hers. Being broody was part of the job. Yes, she saw the less glamorous ailments which came for pregnant women, but she also saw the rewards in the form of gorgeous, happy bundles of fun like Amy.

It increased her yearning for a family of her own, to have chubby babies and do all the things she'd never got to do with her own parents. Baking cookies, teaching them to ride a bike or tie their shoelaces, going to nativity plays and doing the school run. All normal things people took for granted and did out of love, not obligation. Her grandmother had been a substitute for Sophie's parents but, as much as she'd loved her, she had often wished to have her parents there on special occasions. She vowed if she ever did become a mother her children would never feel abandoned or a burden.

That was why she could never pin her future on a man such as Roman, someone who couldn't be relied upon to be a constant source of support. It was the reason she had settled for 'safe' in her relationships to date. Unfortunately, it wasn't possible to have both and though she was enjoying wild passion with Roman it would be fleeting. Eventually she would come to her senses and remember to put her hopes and dreams above her libido. With Roman, the only future she was facing was one with a broken heart and that was a poor choice against the possibility of a stable relationship and a family of her own.

If only she could find a man who excited her as much as he did, minus the commitment-phobia, she might actually have that happy ending everyone else seemed to get.

Roman should have headed back to his place to sleep after the day he'd had. Being on scene at two major RTAs had been stressful, even if the casualties were on their way to recovery.

Except he'd been looking forward to the

end of his shift so he could see Sophie again. They hadn't made plans per se, it wasn't easy with their hectic schedules, but he hadn't been able to stop thinking about last night. If he was honest with himself she'd been on his mind since his last breakup.

Lena had flung a few home truths at him when he had called things off between them before he'd come back to Carey Cove. Comments which had made him take a good hard look at the life he had created for himself. She had accused him of being afraid to put down roots and terrified of getting close to anyone. That he used his career and his 'flighty playboy image' as an excuse to avoid commitment.

Roman had never considered himself to be a coward in his entire life, always one to face a challenge or accept a dare. Where relationships were concerned, though, he began to realise she'd been right. His issues had started with his parents and ended with Sophie French. A mother and father who were so disappointed in him had led him to believe he wasn't good enough for Sophie and even though he had loved her he had sacrificed a future with her to save them both. Staying for her would have meant remaining tied to his family but, more importantly, he would have ended up hurting her, something he would never have intentionally done. Everything he'd done since then had been his attempt to avoid conflict. He wasn't so sure that had been so successful in any capacity.

When the job had come up in Carey Cove he'd imagined it was fate, a chance to see he had done the right thing all those years ago. Except he had been afraid to go and see Sophie and find she had moved on after all, when it seemed he couldn't.

Roman wasn't sure sleeping together was going to do much to help them put the past behind them, but Sophie had seemed so sure that was what she wanted. That giving into their libidos for a short time, ignoring any residual emotions from their teenage years, was exactly what they needed. Well, he wasn't made of stone.

Waking up in her bed for an encore performance had been a bonus, even if he'd had to leave early for work.

Now, instead of returning to his rented, cheerless accommodation, he found himself on the road to Sophie's cottage, the rainbow lights welcoming him in the darkness. He rang the bell and waited, his breath hovering in the frosty air as he listened for the sound of footsteps to confirm she was at home.

'Roman? What are you doing here?' She answered the door swamped in an oversized cardigan and wearing fluffy pink slipper boots, clearly not expecting company tonight.

'I…er…' It didn't seem in keeping with their casual agreement to admit he couldn't wait to see her again.

'Just thought I'd swing by on my way home.'

'Uh-huh. Is this what a booty call looks like?' she asked, arms folded, eyebrow raised, and her mouth curved up into a smirk.

As much as he wanted to say yes and cart her back off to bed, she still deserved more than that. The truth was he simply wanted to spend more time with her. If this was the last time he came back to Carey Cove or their final chance to be together, he wanted to get to know her again. For however short a time they had.

'I thought you might like to go out somewhere.' He leaned casually against the doorframe so it didn't seem like a big deal for him to be here.

'A date?'

'Yes. No. I don't know. We can stay in if you prefer?' He waggled his eyebrows in such an overtly suggestive manner it made her laugh.

'It depends on what else is on offer.'

He had to think quickly and free his mind of all thoughts involving Sophie naked, lying beneath him.

'I don't think anything's going to top that, but if we're talking outdoor pursuits, I thought we could pay a visit to the Christmas market over in Hodden. We could get some mulled wine, buy some handmade tacky decorations and sit on Santa's lap.'

'How could I refuse an offer like that?' She reached for her coat hanging in the hall and replaced her slippers with a sturdy pair of boots. With a swirl of her scarf around her neck, she closed the door, ready to follow him. He was grateful she didn't want to play games with him and was quite happy to go along with him. Any other woman he had spurned in the past might have sought payback or played hard to get. Sophie was still the same honest person she had always been when it came to her feelings. He was the one who had issues in that department.

They walked the short distance towards the nearby village, the festive hub glowing in the darkness of the winter evening. Even in the icy air there was an undercurrent of heat between them, as if the small talk about their working day and this trip out was the foreplay before another amazing night in bed. He certainly hoped so, although he was content merely to be in her company.

Since coming back he'd had to start over making friends and getting to know his colleagues. With Sophie it was so easy to be himself. She was familiar and welcoming. Everything coming home should have felt like to him. Now they had reconnected as adults she was even sexier and more fun than he remembered. It almost made him regret walking away all those years ago, though he had done it for all the right reasons and made a life for himself away from the disapproving stares of his parents. Even if he was starting to see that it was not as fulfilling as he had once thought. If he had been truly happy jumping from one job and relationship to another he would never have felt the pull back here, to Sophie.

She pulled her scarf up further until only her eyes were visible behind the shield of forest-green wool. As tempted as he was to pull her close and share his body heat with her, it might have been a bit presumptuous. She might not want their temporary relationship status to be public knowledge. He was sure she wouldn't want to start explaining it or their history to her friends and patients.

Roman played it safe and led her over to one of the log cabin-style stalls selling hot beverages.

'Hot chocolate, spiced cider or mulled wine?' he asked, scanning the menu.

'Ooh, a spiced cider, I think.'

He decided on the same and handed a cup to Sophie. With her hands wrapped around the cup she closed her eyes and breathed in the rising steam. 'It smells like Christmas.'

'Tastes like it too,' he added after taking a sip.

'This whole place looks like the cover of a Christmas novel.'

'Haven't you been here before? I thought this would have been your idea of heaven.' As a child Sophie had been almost obsessive about the season, whereas he could have happily let Christmas pass by without a celebration. It had only brought more arguments in his household, his brothers getting the better presents and Roman deemed ungrateful for the gifts they'd thought he should want.

They strolled past the stalls selling hotdogs and cupcakes, the savoury and sweet aromas making him hungry.

'I'm usually too tired after work and

Christmas hasn't really been the same for me since Gran died. I go through the motions but it's like I'm trying to force it these days.'

It would be a shame for Sophie to be as miserable as he usually was at this time of year and Roman was determined to give her a good night out.

'Tonight we are going to reawaken your Christmas spirit. So drink up and get your Christmas jingle on, Sophie French.' At least she had kept up with the Christmas decorating and baking and he was sure she simply needed a nudge to truly rediscover her love of the season. To get back to the Sophie he used to know.

'Oh, yeah? How do you reckon you're going to do that, Roman Callahan?' She nudged him with her elbow as he was knocking back the rest of his cider so it dribbled down his chin and splashed onto his coat.

'I'm so sorry.' She pulled off her glove and began to pat at his chest. That slight touch was enough to spark vivid memories of last night, sending heat coursing through Roman's entire being.

'It's fine. I'm sure we can put our heads together and come up with something to make you feel warm and cosy.' He held Sophie's gaze and saw the flash of desire, matching his own. It would be the most natural thing in the world to take her in his arms and kiss her senseless, and that was exactly what he wanted to do. Except he couldn't be certain that Sophie would be pleased about doing that in front of the rest of the village. Instead, he took a step back and brushed himself down, composing himself to get rid of that husky hunger in his voice.

'There's an ice rink. What better way to get us in the Christmas mood?'

'Sliding about on the ice, falling on my backside and potentially having my fingers amputated by a sharp blade when someone skates over my hand? Sure, it screams Christmas.' She rolled her eyes at him, the heat of the moment cooled by her cynicism.

'Come on. It'll be fun.' Plus they would be in a crowd so there was less chance of him succumbing to his desire to kiss her until they were somewhere more private.

'There's a very good reason I've never had broken bones or stitches. I avoid activities where there's a chance I'll get hurt.'

Yet she had entered into this arrangement with him. Roman thought it was time for Sophie to explore a little further beyond her comfort zone. Then when he inevitably moved on she would be ready to do the same. For as long as he had known her, Sophie had played it safe. All the more remarkable that she had suggested a no-strings fling with him. She knew he was anything but the reliable option. If she had any misconceived notion that they had a long-term future ahead she was sure to come back down to earth with a bump when she remembered who she was dealing with. Roman Callahan always disappointed those close to him. That was why he didn't stay in one place for too long. Whether that was so he didn't witness the fallout or to pre-empt it he couldn't be certain.

Perhaps he should never have come back. It had been a reckless idea to seek Sophie out and definitely a bang-his-head-off-the-wall mistake to sleep with her. However, the deed was done and never to be forgotten. If anything, he wanted to repeat the mistake over and over again. The best he could hope for was damage control and that started with helping Sophie take baby steps onto the ice.

'Don't you trust me, Sophie?' Roman held out his hand, waiting for her to accompany him to the rink.

She knew it was a dare, a test to determine

if she trusted him not to hurt her. No. Not when it came to matters of the heart, but she was trying to play it cool and pretend that casual hook-ups were nothing more to her than convenient.

Sophie slapped her hand in his, accepting the challenge. It wasn't as though she had gone into this with her eyes closed. She knew the score and was prepared to take the risk to reap the reward. The same could be applied here when it meant spending more time with Roman.

'If I lose a limb I'm blaming you.'

'Don't worry, I know first aid and a very good surgeon.'

'You're so reassuring,' she muttered as he got their skates from the booth at the side of the rink.

'I promise I'll be with you all the way,' Roman told her as they laced up their skates.

Sophie had no control over the extra beat her heart gave, deliberately misinterpreting his meaning. If only that entailed longer than it would take them to lap the ice she wouldn't be wishing for insurance to cover future heartache.

She stood up on her blades and wobbled. Roman reached out and grabbed her.

'Great. I'm not even on the ice yet and I'm a liability.'

'I've got you.' He took her by the hand and helped her teeter over to the edge of the rink without as much as a waver in his gait.

'Let me know which bit of this is supposed to be fun.' Other than Roman having his arm around her, she didn't see what there was to be gained from this.

He laughed, not put off in the slightest by her blatant cynicism and determination not to enjoy this.

'Just put one foot in front of the other and keep moving,' he helpfully suggested as her foot met the ice and immediately slid from beneath her.

'Maybe I should get one of those penguin helpers.' She saw the other newbie ice skaters pushing around solid fibreglass penguin figures, relying on them for stability. It didn't matter it was mostly under-tens using them, it had to be more dignified than being held up by another adult.

'You'll be flying around the ice in no time. Relax. Focus on moving forward instead of what your feet are, or aren't, doing.' He put his hands on her hips and pushed her forward so she was gliding across the ice.

'How are you such an expert?' It was infuriating that they were not both starting out at the same level. She was at a distinct disadvantage already, seeing he could move with more grace than her baby deer learning to walk impression.

'I've dated a lot, and you know ice-skating at Christmas is romantic. I've seduced a woman or two with my fancy footwork.' He skated around her, then spun around on the spot before coming back to keep her upright.

Sophie knew he was teasing her but she could hear the truth in his words. It wasn't a surprise to find there had been other women. It was the fact that she wasn't special that called to that emptiness inside her. This was Roman's *modus operandi* when it came to casual relationships. It somewhat dimmed the romantic glow of the evening. Regardless that he was doing this for her benefit, to make her think there was more to this than a tumble in bed.

'You don't need to impress me, Roman. I'm a sure thing. We don't have to go along with this farce, and I certainly don't have to humiliate myself in the process.' While he was boasting about past lovers she was trying not to fall on her backside in front of tiny tots and gangly teens. None of this was bringing her joy, only misery burning the back of her eyeballs.

Roman swung around and took her face in his hands. 'Hey. No tears. I just wanted to spend time with you tonight and I thought ice-skating was one thing we could do together. If you're really hating it that much we can do something else. I think there's a bucking bronco dressed as a reindeer if you'd rather do that?'

That made her smile, albeit a quivery one. Deep down she knew he cared, and that had to be enough because it was never going to be any more than that.

She sucked up her self-pity and got her flirty alter-ego back on. 'Now that is a ride I'd rather do in the privacy of my own home.'

The concern etched on Roman's face slowly changed into a much sexier grin. Deciding to capitalise on the moment, Sophie gave him a quick peck on the lips. She could tell she had caught him by surprise by the shocked expression he wore but if his reaction was to be believed he wasn't averse to her spontaneity.

He came back for more, returning her brief kiss with a leisurely, full-lipped experience. Not only was it hot enough to melt her and the ice she was balancing on, it drew a few whistles and a comment from one not so impressed skater.

'Not the time or the place,' she sniffed as she jostled them on her way past, knocking the couple off-balance. Roman fought valiantly to stay standing, refusing to let go of Sophie.

She was tempted to shout, *Save yourself*, as her skates slid back and forth, failing to find traction, but the hard fall on her backside knocked the words out of her. Roman swore before tumbling down beside her.

After the initial pain and shock of her ungraceful landing, Sophie saw the funny side of them sprawled on the ice and began to giggle. It was apparently contagious as Roman joined in.

'Hey, you two. Get a room. It'll be much warmer than lying down there.' Kiara Baxter from Carey House was looking down at her with a knowing smile.

Before Sophie managed to formulate a retort her colleague was skating away hand in hand with Lucas, her other half.

Seeing her embarrassment catching up with her, Roman got to his feet and helped her to do the same. 'Do you want to get out of here?'

Sophie looked around, saw other couples

hand in hand and tottering their way around. So she had fallen and survived, her colleague had seen and the world hadn't ended. She had a bruised backside and her clothes were wet through. It seemed silly not to stick around for the rewards of her efforts when she had already endured her worst fears.

'We've already paid for the session.' She took his hand. 'I might even be having fun.'

'Yes!' he exclaimed a little too loudly and punched the air. It was true, he did know how to show her a good time in and out of bed.

With renewed determination to conquer the ice and her irrational fear, Sophie followed Roman's tutelage until she was able to take a few steps on her own. Even if she did throw herself back into his arms after her initial solo success, it gained her a touching kiss on the top of her head and a cuddle, making it all worth it.

When their time was up she had mastered a wobbly solo skate and was glowing. As indicated by her red nose and rosy cheeks, which she caught sight of in the funhouse mirrors nearby. She was also cold and hungry.

'Hot dog?' Roman asked as they passed the stall, reading her mind.

They sat down to eat at a nearby table, where they were able to watch the ice-skaters and market-goers. Seeing families enjoying the evening together inevitably made her think not only about her parents but Roman's too.

'Would you ever think about reaching out to your family? They must be keen to find out how you are.'

'You'd think so,' he scoffed.

'Whatever happened, surely you can work it out? You could get to spend time with them. Not all of us are that blessed.' Although Sophie's outlook was vastly different to that of her mother and father, she would give anything to have family around her again, especially at this time of year. She couldn't fathom what could have happened for Roman to completely divorce himself from his.

'That's the reason I never told you the way things were at home for me. I knew it wouldn't be fair to complain when you had lost your own parents. Perhaps if I had explained what was going on it would have helped you understand why I had to leave and why I never intended to come back.'

Sophie suddenly lost her appetite, tossing the remnants of her hot dog back in the mustard-covered cardboard tray on the table. It was true they'd never talked about Roman's home life, and she had assumed it was because he lived the perfect childhood there in the grand house, wanting for nothing. She had been too caught up in her own grief, too self-centred to even think there was something wrong at home. If she had stopped to think she might have realised all was not well. Clearly, Roman had also thought she had no interest in his problems or he would have shared them with her. They had been close but obviously not as much as she had imagined if he couldn't confide in her.

'I'm sorry you didn't think you could talk to me.'

'It's not your fault, Soph. I was a privileged teen, you were an orphan. I didn't think I had any right to be unhappy.'

'I'm listening now. What was so bad you thought you had to leave for ever?' At the time she had believed she would never see him again and she was the cause. With neither assumption true, she wanted to know the real reason Roman had been driven away and what, if anything, she could do to help. If it was something which could be resolved it might make him reconsider staying. For his own peace of mind. It certainly wouldn't make her life any easier if he hung around longer than their fling lasted.

Roman sighed, though he had managed to finish his snack. He scrunched up his rubbish and tossed it into the nearby bin. 'They wanted me to follow them into the family business, I wanted to go to medical school.'

'Surely that's all in the past though? You made the right choice and you have a good, admirable career.' Sophie could see how that might have transpired into a battle of wills at the time, but with so much time passed his parents should have got over the decision he'd made. They might not have thought of him as an adult at the time, capable of making his own life choices, but he was now. Plus, whatever they role they had envisaged him taking in the company would have been filled long ago. She saw no reason for any lingering resentment to prevent a reunion, merely stubborn pride on both sides.

'You would think so, but they made it clear they thought they knew best. Anything less than taking the reins in the company wasn't worthy of the family name. My brothers are both heading up international branches of the company and, though we do occasionally keep in contact, I haven't seen them in years.' Even talking about his family was clearly making his blood pressure rise, the colour in his cheeks coming from more than the cold weather.

'This was the argument you had before going to medical school, but you hinted at some ongoing problems.' It was important for her to dig deeper to find out what had had such an effect on him. To better understand Roman and their relationship. She owed him, and herself, that much.

'Nothing I did was ever good enough for them. I wasn't the son they wanted. My brothers conformed to the ideals they had, and they couldn't understand why I wouldn't. I insisted on being my own person. As you know.' The nod to his exploits growing up, including dangerous stunts he'd undertaken to get a rise out of her and whatever audience he had around him at the time, at least brought a smile to his face again.

'I may not have always agreed with or liked the things you did, but I learned to accept that you doing crazy stuff was part of our friendship. It was who you were and I lo… I loved that you were your own person.' A slip of the tongue almost gave away her true feelings and if Roman was afraid of anything it was expressing real emotions. Nothing would put him off the idea of this convenient dalliance more than knowing she had real feelings for him. Something she was desperately trying to ignore herself.

'Me being me was not acceptable to them and they let me know it at every opportunity.' The memories of which were setting his jaw to stone as he ground his teeth together. Sophie wondered if it was time for a change in topic to prevent him from getting stuck in the darkness of his childhood.

'I'm so sorry, Roman. You were so outgoing and confident I never considered you had so many issues at home. I always wondered why you took an interest in me, the quiet wallflower.'

'We might have had very different circumstances, but I think I recognised that same sadness and isolation in you when you lost your parents.'

'I always thought it was pity for the poor orphan. Thank you, I needed someone, other than my gran, of course, to remind me there was life outside of my grief. Even if you did worry me half to death with some of your stunts.' Her fingernails had been bitten down to the quick watching him jump off the school roof or diving from the cliffs into the sea, whatever needlessly dangerous dare he undertook because he felt like it.

'Sorry. I didn't do those things solely to annoy you. I knew I could do them and it gave me a sense of achievement. Praise from my peers was intoxicating when it was something I didn't get at home.'

Sophie found it difficult to have any empathy for his parents, even though they had all lost Roman ten years ago. She knew better than anyone that a person couldn't be forced to become someone else simply because it suited another person's agenda. They had pushed him away, and if they weren't remorseful in the slightest about their actions they could lose him for ever.

'I just worried about you. I'd lost my parents to all of their crazy risk-taking. They abandoned me to pursue that lifestyle, didn't give a thought to the daughter left behind. I think that's why I went the opposite route, to keep myself safe. The one time I did take a risk and kissed you, you abandoned me too. I wasn't enough for my parents or you. My broken heart taught me I'd been right all along to protect myself.'

Roman hung his head. 'I'm sorry if I made you feel like I didn't want you. Believe it or not, I was trying to do the right thing. I knew I would only let you down the way I'd been letting my parents down my whole life. It was never about not wanting you, Sophie.' He reached out and brushed a strand of hair away from her face.

'And now?' It took all her strength to ask, putting her heart on the line for a second time and tempting another rejection, but she needed to know once and for all.

Roman arched an eyebrow before taking both of her hands in his. 'I still want you, Sophie French.'

Okay, it was not a declaration of undying love, but it still made her squeal inside. It was the most she could hope for when they had spent so much time apart. Who knew, maybe that physical need might transform into something more. Did she want that? Probably. Was it asking for trouble? Definitely. The trick was to not let Roman think that she was conning him into something more than he had agreed to.

She stood up and held out her hand. 'In that case, what are we doing wasting time out here in the cold when I have a lovely warm bed for you at home?'

CHAPTER FIVE

'HEY, SOPH. HOW'S THINGS?'

Roman's voice on the hands-free speaker filled Sophie's car, making her day a little brighter.

'Hi. I'm just on my way to see a patient. Is something wrong?' It wasn't long since they'd parted and usually he texted her during the day, knowing she was often too busy to take a call. Lucky for both of them, she was visiting one of their mums-to-be who lived a little way out of civilisation, giving her more driving time and an opportunity to speak to Roman.

Hearing him made it feel as though he were more present, so she didn't have time to miss him. Goodness, she had it bad. She had tried to fool herself that she could be with him and not lose her head or her heart, but the reality was quite different. Sleeping with Roman only gave her more reason to love him, when she knew it was a wasted emotion. He'd only gone along with this because she had promised it would mean nothing to her and he could move on soon with a clear conscience. It wasn't his fault he had made her fall for him even deeper, and he didn't ever have to know. She didn't want this to end now they had finally acknowledged there was something more between them than teenage crushes and friendly banter. They might only have a limited time together, but she wanted to explore their relationship further. As far as Roman would allow.

His chuckle echoed around her, reaching right into her chest to give her heart a little squeeze. 'You know me too well. I'm afraid I have some bad news. I'll have to cancel our dinner date tonight.'

Sophie's good mood evaporated. The thought of him cooking the famous Spaghetti Bolognese he had boasted about for her and taking her into his bed later that night had been fuelling her day so far. For every backache and urine infection she had dealt with today, she had envisaged pasta and a naked Roman waiting for her to get her through. It was unnerving how quickly he had become such a huge part of her life again.

'Why?' She tried not to whine like a spoiled child upset at not getting her way, even though that was exactly who she was in that moment.

'I'm afraid the flat isn't fit for company. The pipes have burst and flooded the place. I'm here now, paddling in my kitchen. I think because I haven't been home much and haven't had the heating on the pipes froze. I'm sorry, babe.'

It was a horrible thought to imagine his belongings ruined like that and Sophie cursed herself for being so selfish when Roman was having a difficult time.

'Do you need me to come over after work and help clean up? I could bring a takeaway with me if you'd like?'

'No, it's okay, but thanks for the offer. I'm clearing up now. I've turned the water off at the mains, but the plumber can't get here until tomorrow. I'll have to pack a few things and find somewhere to stay for the night.'

'Why don't you stay over at mine?' The words were out and Sophie couldn't take them back, despite cringing into the driving seat once she'd said them, afraid of coming across as too keen and needy. The opposite of how she should play this if she had a chance of convincing Roman she was the sort of woman he was used to being with. One who wouldn't weep and wail when he had gone.

The tell-tale silence made her want to disappear through the floor of the car. When Roman's voice eventually crackled to life again with the stuttering familiarity of a lost connection, for once Sophie was glad the wilds of Cornwall had bad reception.

'Sorry, Roman, I didn't get that. I don't think the signal is great out here.'

'Can you hear me now?'

Once she confirmed she could hear him loud and clear again, his response finally reached her. 'I was just asking if you were sure that was all right.'

She thought about it. What could possibly be bad about offering him a place to stay for one night? The only thing that came to mind was the possibility it could seem a bit too much like having a relationship, but if it was okay with Roman…

'Of course. There's no point in paying for a hotel room when you will likely be staying over at mine anyway.' The offer was not entirely altruistic when she was making sure he would be warming her bed tonight.

'Thanks. I probably will when I can't stop thinking about you and all the things we should be doing to each other right now.' His voice dipped, reaching that part of her aching to have him tonight and every night after.

'When can you come?' She was breathy now with the anticipation of another evening with their naked bodies entwined in her sheets.

'I'll be over as soon as I can. I promise not to bring my pipe and slippers with me, although I will need my toothbrush.' He was teasing her about things becoming too complacent between them already, but Sophie doubted she would ever take him for granted when the nature of their relationship was so precarious. She wouldn't dream of expecting him to move in long-term when that was the one thing she could be sure would never happen. Tonight was an emergency situation and it was convenient for both of them. Much like their current arrangement.

'Yeah, I don't want your dragon breath in the morning,' she replied, keeping things light. This was no big deal. Just Roman Callahan moving into her cottage for an adult sleepover.

Roman's day had been a washout. He'd spent it dealing with his landlord, the insurance company and the plumber. Thankfully, there was only superficial damage to the furniture and his personal possessions had been largely unaffected by the indoor deluge of his apartment. However, it had been a headache he could have done without. Now he was looking forward to being with Sophie and forgetting, even for a few hours, that it had ever happened.

Now he was on his way, though, with his overnight bag packed, he was beginning to wonder if things weren't a little too cosy. She had been his first call after dealing with the emergency, relying on her counsel and support to help him through something he would usually have sorted without a second thought. It was as though he was using any excuse to spend time with her, to the extent he was already moving in. Albeit temporarily.

With any new partner it usually took him a while before he even spent the night, never mind bring his belongings with him. He didn't want to give anyone the wrong idea about the possibility of a future relationship and be tied down. Both parties maintained their own space, then there was no chance of any confusion.

Of course these were extraordinary circumstances, with the problem at his apartment and knowing Sophie for so long, but it still rang alarm bells that he was doing this already. That he was looking forward to making himself at home in the cottage. He could see why she had been reluctant to change anything there since her grandmother had died when it was just as comforting as ever to him too being somewhere so familiar and safe. A dangerous position for someone like him to be in.

Once the initial euphoria of great sex wore off he might need a little space from her, just so he could get his head straight. Start relying on his common sense rather than his libido to guide him through the minefield of a casual relationship with his childhood sweetheart.

After tonight, of course. He'd been looking forward to sharing dinner and bed with Sophie too much to deny himself the pleasure at the last minute. He wasn't a masochist.

Sophie had the door open before he had even stopped the car. Simply seeing her face was a reward after a fraught day. She calmed him and reminded him that life didn't always have to be lived at full pelt. He was beginning to enjoy the simple pleasures everyone else took for granted. Before his return to Carey Cove, Roman hadn't seen the appeal in rushing home after work just to sit around watching TV when there were so many more activities available out there to try. He filled his spare time with outdoor leisure pursuits or planning his next adventure holiday. Now, there was nothing he wanted more than to chill out with his feet up, simply enjoying Sophie's company.

'Hey, you.' He kissed her on the cheek and set his bag down in the hall. It had all the markings of the very domestic scene he'd been avoiding his entire life. The only thing worse than finding himself in the middle of it was the fact he liked it. Perhaps that was what he feared more than commitment itself. That if he did find himself settling down with someone he would be leaving himself open to the same criticisms he'd faced at home, breaking his spirit and expecting him to be someone he wasn't. He couldn't go through all of that again, more so with Sophie. It was probably better that they did leave this as a no-strings fling and remember it as a happy memory than to end up resenting each other, the way he and his parents had.

'Rough day?' Sophie took his jacket and

hung it in the hall. He followed her into the kitchen, where the table was set for two with soft music playing in the background.

Roman sighed out his frustrations at the devastation caused in his apartment, glad he had someone to vent to. 'A lot of hassle I could have done without, but hopefully it will all be done by tomorrow. I might have to do a spot of redecorating but at least I caught it before it was a complete washout. Now, what smells so good in here, apart from you?'

He grabbed Sophie for a quick cuddle and buried his nose in her hair to inhale that sweet scent of vanilla and strawberries which had come to smell like home to him.

'I thought I'd cook since you had a good excuse to get out of it tonight.'

She handed him a glass of wine and pulled out a chair for him to sit down.

'I could get used to being spoiled like this,' he said, giving her a soft kiss on the mouth to thank her for all of her effort. He had forgotten what it was like to have someone looking out for him, to be there when he needed them, making things right when everything seemed to be going wrong. Just like when they were kids and he'd turned to Sophie after clashing with his parents and needing a place of refuge. She was still his sanctuary.

'Oh, this isn't for your benefit. I was just really in the mood for some Spag Bol,' Sophie teased as she dished up the home-cooked meal he hadn't been expecting tonight.

'And how was your day, dear?' he asked with a hint of sarcasm as he tucked into his pasta, slipping into the role of the nineteen-fifties husband this domestic scene seemed to require of him.

Sophie grinned. 'I started with the walk-in clinic for mums-to-be at Carey House, did my rounds in the car, weighed some babies and came home to make dinner in time for my man coming over.'

Roman knew she was kidding around but the more this began to look and feel like a comfy relationship, the more uncomfortable he was becoming. Yes, they were joking around about the situation they had found themselves in tonight, but the ease with which he was accepting the situation was what made it unpalatable. A fling should not include too many prearranged overnight stays nor cosy homemade dinners for two. When he thought about it, his motivations were all wrong. This thing between them was only supposed to have been about sex, not some fake marriage situation.

He dropped the forkful of food he was no longer hungry for. 'What are we doing, Sophie?'

She frowned, then smiled before answering what should have been a rhetorical question. He knew exactly what they were doing and why they shouldn't be doing it.

'Er...we're having dinner. Did the water short-circuit your brain today?'

'No, I mean this.' He gestured to the lit candle in the middle of the table and to his bag, sitting in the hallway waiting to be unpacked.

Now Sophie abandoned her meal and pushed her plate away. 'Look, Roman, you needed somewhere to stay and I offered you a bed for the night. I was cooking dinner anyway and I knew you'd had a rough day. There was no great plot to trap you into a life of domesticity.' She was ticked off at him and rightly so, when all she had done was be there for him. Roman was the one with the problem, he knew that. Commitment and intimacy issues ensured that the second he had anything resembling happiness in his life, he had to question it.

'I just don't want you thinking that this is

anything other than a fling or that tonight is more than a favour.'

'Oh, get over yourself, Roman Callahan. What makes you think that you're such a great catch I would want to give up my independence and become the little housewife, waiting for you to come home from work to give my life meaning? I've been looking after myself for a long time. If you don't want to stay the night, fine. We'll screw and you can book yourself into a hotel room for the night if you'd prefer.' The pink spots in her cheeks were glowing brighter with every harsh word she threw at him. He hadn't been prepared for her reaction to be so, well, visceral. Roman couldn't be sure if it was that display of undisguised passionate anger or her denial that she needed any form of relationship with him outside the bedroom, but he wanted her right now.

'Maybe I would.' He stood up and leaned across the table. Sophie mirrored him, then all at once they were kissing, mouths and tongues clashing as they gave in to the electricity arcing between them and causing this sudden power surge.

Head buzzing with thoughts only of having her, he cleared the table with one swipe of his arm, dishes and pasta sauce spilling everywhere.

'I'll replace it,' he told her as the smashed crockery hit the tiled floor.

'It doesn't matter,' she gasped, crawling across the table so they could reach each other more easily.

Roman knew this was about asserting the nature of their 'fling', for both of them, but he was still hot for her after the way she had spoken to him so vehemently and honestly. Sophie wasn't afraid of saying what she thought and she didn't play games. She was exactly who he needed.

Sophie's heart was fit to burst it was pumping so hard and fast against her ribcage. For a moment she'd thought Roman was going to end things there and then, simply because she had cooked him a meal. Now raw passion had turned her kitchen into a den of iniquity, and she didn't care. Yes, her outburst had been prompted by fear of losing him and that desperate need to convince him she wasn't going to get clingy, but now it was all about the sex. Just the way he wanted and what she had agreed to.

She was sitting on the edge of the table now, Roman pushing her dress up her thighs and pulling off her panties. When she'd been standing making dinner she would never have guessed it would have led to something so wild and erotic. She didn't let her lips leave his as they both worked to push his trousers and boxers out of the way, but there was one thing they had to be mindful of.

'Condom,' she gasped, aching to have him inside her but also fearful of the consequences if they weren't careful. A pregnancy was the one thing guaranteed to see him running for the hills.

Once contraception was taken care of, Roman pushed her gently back onto the table and pulled her along the table towards him so he was standing between her legs. She was ready for him, aroused by the sheer notion of what they were about to do on her kitchen table.

He filled her with one flex of his hips and Sophie stretched out, hands above her head, surrendering her body to his will. His grunts of effort and satisfaction as he pushed into her matched Sophie's. It was bliss every time they joined together. Here, she was content. There was no pressure to mind what she was saying in case she scared him off when she knew he was every bit as happy to be doing this.

With every thrust they rose and clung together, driving towards their mutual goal, their bodies in tune even if their minds remained on different things. They fitted perfectly together, snug and right. Some day Roman might come to see that.

Despite their short-lived tiff over their arrangement and insistence they were only together for sex, Roman had spent every night since in Sophie's bed. Minus the luggage which had made him question their status in the first place.

He knew they were veering into dangerous territory, and it disturbed him more than his usual adrenaline-fuelled exploits. It was making him question his true feelings as much as Sophie's. He was becoming too used to climbing into her bed at the end of a shift and waking up beside her in the morning. There was nothing like winding down from a stress-filled day and coming home to make love to her. When he was with Sophie he didn't need to be searching for the next daredevil stunt. He was content in her company, and he was sure she felt the same. Except when they were having sex, when 'content' turned to 'mind-blowing'.

The revelations about Sophie's teenage

mindset had weighed on his mind since the night they had gone ice-skating. If he was guilty of taking too many risks, she had taken the opposite path, afraid of taking any. He hadn't realised the lasting impact the loss of her parents had had on her, or how much it would shape her life. If he had, he might have handled their separation with more care. His intention had never been for her to feel abandoned or unwanted, he had experienced enough of that himself to ever inflict it on anyone else. Now that he knew the truth, he had a duty to rectify his mistakes and undo the belief Sophie had harboured for so long which prevented her from living her life to the fullest.

They had grown closer since that night when they had opened up about their families and the issues which had crept into their relationship. While he was enjoying it, it was important for them both to remember this thing between them was not for ever. He hadn't changed from who he was, and Sophie would be disappointed if she believed otherwise. This time, when they parted ways, he wanted to make sure it was a mutual, pain-free exercise. He hoped that if he was able to help her move further out of her comfort zone she would realise she didn't need him or anyone else to validate her.

Although she'd been resistant even to the idea of ice-skating, it had not taken much to coax her into participating and eventually enjoying it. He intended to get her more involved in the sort of activities he did outside of work, to get her blood pumping and remind her she was alive. That she had not died along with her parents or her grandmother.

Today he was making another surprise Santa visit at the local village fair and Sophie was waiting for him on the ground below with the rest of the crowd. Abseiling down from a helicopter was part of his job and not something which made him nervous at all. However, he knew she would be watching and worrying, and he wanted to prove to her it wasn't necessary. That she could enjoy the spectacle without anticipating the worst might happen.

'Ready when you are.' He signalled to the pilot before donning his long white curly beard and red felt hat.

He leaned out and waved to the crowd below, the cheers drowned out by the sound of the helicopter blades above his head. After making sure his safety harness was secure, he grabbed hold of his sack of toys and leaned back. He tried not to think too much about Sophie, whose heart would be in her mouth, watching his descent, focusing instead on lowering out of the helicopter. They were hovering above the middle of the village green, the families below spreading outwards to leave a wide circle for him to drop into.

He hit the ground and quickly disentangled the safety rope. 'Ho, ho, ho.'

A round of applause erupted around him, giving Roman that sense of satisfaction that he had achieved something. People were happy to see him, even if it was because they were expecting a gift and a promise that he would bring more on Christmas Eve.

As he shook hands and said hello on his way over to the grotto they had set up in the community centre, he was scanning the assembled throng for Sophie. He spotted her standing on her own, her hood pulled up to protect her from the elements and giving him the thumbs-up with a grin on her face. It was a start and a relief to see her as pleased as the rest of the crowd welcoming his safe arrival. Fingers crossed, she would be equally happy when they went their separate ways because she still needed someone who could give her more than he ever could.

'Are you in the queue?' a mother holding a baby in her arms and a toddler by the hand asked Sophie inside the community centre.

'No, sorry. Go on ahead.' She'd been day-dreaming about Roman and inadvertently got caught up in the rush of children hoping to see Santa. Moving from the hallway to the main hall gave her more breathing space, as well as the chance to see him up close.

This past week with him had been glori-ous and eye-opening. Not only were they having the most amazing sex, but they were really getting to know each other on a deeper level than ever before. She was learning something new about him every day. And herself. With the confidence he had in his abilities, she'd had to trust he knew what he was doing by dropping in today by helicop-ter. That fear for him would probably never leave her, but Roman always landed on his feet. Today she'd had to ignore that urge to look away and simply appreciate the joy he was bringing to the children with his un-usual arrival.

'He's great with the kids, isn't he?' Nya,

dressed in a festive Mrs Claus outfit, walked up beside her.

'He is. Everyone is leaving with a smile on their face.' She watched the families troop out of the grotto with the children clutching their presents and chattering excitedly about the time they'd got to spend with Father Christmas.

'How are things going between you two?'

'Good.' She didn't have to say any more than that, sure the smile on her face said it all.

'So you wouldn't mind working together?'

Nya's question drew Sophie's gaze away from Roman and added a frown. 'What do you mean? If it involves jumping out of helicopters, it's a definite no.'

'Don't worry, it's nothing medical-related or airborne. Unless the helicopter crew come back with an emergency. No, we need someone to take the pictures. Our photographer is a little under the weather and wants a break.'

'I'm not an expert by any means. Isn't there someone else who could stand in?' Sophie didn't want the responsibility of potentially ruining the memory of someone's visit with a blurry snap.

'Don't worry, it's an instant camera. All you have to do is snap away. I'd do it myself, but I have to organise the queue and keep the kiddies happy. You know it's all about the present anyway.' Nya laughed and led Sophie over to the grotto without giving her the opportunity to say no.

Considering the lack of budget and space, those who had built Santa's toy room had done a good job. An archway cobbled together with plywood and covered with red tissue paper and a layer of cotton wool gave the illusion of a little house. Roman sat on a huge chair inside, surrounded by colourfully wrapped gifts, with a little boy sitting on his lap.

Nya handed her the camera. 'Point and click. Good luck.'

'Thanks,' Sophie mumbled to her back as she had already exited the small space.

Roman, who was listening to the seemingly never-ending Christmas list of his little visitor, raised his eyebrows when he saw Sophie coming to join him.

She held up the camera and shrugged.

'I will see what I can do for you, Matthew. Now, here's your present and if you look into the camera Miss French will take a photo for you to keep too.'

'Say "Christmas",' Sophie encouraged to get a smile from the child and once she was sure she had both of them looking straight at the camera she pressed the button.

Matthew's mother came to collect him and marvel at the car set he had enthusiastically unwrapped the second he had bounced off Santa's knee.

'Don't forget your photograph.' Sophie handed over the now developed pic, which had caught the subjects perfectly. She was pleased to have been part of the moment.

Once the couple had moved on, Roman stood up and came over to her. 'What on earth are you doing here? Not that I'm complaining. I just didn't expect to see you until later.'

'Nya strong-armed me into filling in for your photographer. Apparently he wasn't feeling very well.'

'It might be the heat, with so many people packed in here. I know I'm melting under this fat suit.' Roman patted his fake belly. He looked cute, regardless of the extra weight he was carrying and the big beard hiding his handsome face.

'Come here.' Sophie fished a handkerchief out of her bag and dabbed at the beads of sweat on his brow.

The costume and the crowd outside the grotto no longer existed as she looked into his eyes. He too appeared to have forgotten where he was as he leaned towards her, his gaze trained on her mouth.

She put a finger to his lips. 'I think it might cause a scandal if Father Christmas is seen kissing one of his helpers.'

'Later?' It sounded like more of a promise than a question and only made Sophie wish more than ever that they were alone.

'Later.' She gave him a wink, suggesting they would be doing more than kissing.

He went back to his chair in time for Nya to chaperone another young visitor into the grotto.

'This is Alice, Santa, she's a little bit shy.' Nya held hands with the child, who was reluctant to get any closer to Roman.

'Hi, Alice. What can I do for you today?' He knelt down on the floor beside the little girl, his voice soft and unthreatening.

Alice turned and buried her head in Nya's skirts, the experience clearly too much for her.

'There's no need to be frightened. Father Christmas only wants to give you a present,' Nya coaxed to no avail.

Roman held his hand up. 'It's okay. I'm not going to force her to talk to me, but I don't know how we're going to find out what she wants as a gift…'

He gave an exaggerated sigh and reached for some of the wrapped parcels. 'I wonder if she would like a toy car? A skipping rope? Maybe a teddy bear?'

The last option managed to turn the little girl's head.

'Would you like a Christmas teddy bear, Amy?' Roman held out the small parcel, still kneeling on the ground and putting no pressure on her to follow the usual protocol when visiting Santa.

It was enough to tempt Amy into reaching out to accept the gift. When the glimmer of a smile crossed her lips, Sophie immediately caught the moment on film. It wasn't the traditional Santa picture but as she watched it develop before her eyes she knew it was every bit as precious as all the other memories which had been captured tonight. As confirmed by the parents who rushed up afterwards to commend them for their efforts with their daughter.

'Thank you for being so patient with her. She's shy but we're encouraging her to mix a bit more before she goes to school. We were pleased when she took Mrs Claus's hand, but the fact she actually interacted with Santa is just wonderful and we have a photograph to remember the moment.' Amy's mother clutched the snap to her chest whilst her little girl was happily showing off her newly unwrapped teddy to her father in the background.

'You're very welcome.' Sophie accepted the praise on behalf of them all and promised to pass on the compliment.

She had been impressed by Roman's interaction with the child too. For someone who seemed to rush at life headlong he had taken his time with Amy, patient until she'd felt comfortable with him. It set Sophie's mind to wondering what he would be like as a father. Compassionate and kind, yet the adventurous sort of parent who would take his kids camping and open their minds to the whole world around them. The only flaw being he might not stick around long-term. Just like her parents. Personally, she would never willingly subject another child to a life of uncertainty.

Only then did she realise she was adding herself into that picture of Roman's potential future family. He had never even said he loved her. Not when they were teenagers and certainly not recently. Although she had never spoken the words aloud, her love for him had been there in her thoughts and actions. Even now, despite her attempts not to admit it to herself, she knew that love for Roman Callahan was burning bright.

If only he was the sort of man who wanted to settle down and have a family she might have been truly happy. Then again, she'd been with men who wanted that, who'd offered her stability and safety and it hadn't satisfied her. Perhaps she would only ever love risk-takers who went against every instinct in protecting her heart. It was possible Roman Callahan was the only man she would ever love. Either way, she knew she was doomed to have her heart broken again. The most she could wish for was more time with him, all the while pretending that it could last for ever.

Once all the gifts had been distributed and the children had gone, Roman was keen to change out of his costume. And get to kiss Sophie without the fear of traumatising the local children.

'Thanks for stepping in. Maybe next time we can talk you into sky-diving, dressed as Rudolph.'

'Don't push it, Santa.' Sophie tugged gently on his beard, and he could tell she was as keen as he was for him to get disrobed.

'I'm just going to change into something more comfortable. I won't be long.' He set off, waving goodbye to everyone, careful not to let anyone see him disappear into the changing rooms so he could take off the outfit and not spoil the illusion for anyone.

He was used to doing these events, but he knew Sophie didn't engage in a lot of community activities outside of work. It had taken him by surprise to see her happily snapping away and helping him wrangle some of the more restless toddlers into sitting for their photographs. She had shared with him her reasons for holding back a huge part of herself, but with a little nudge she could be encouraged to step into the unknown. Taking photographs in a Christmas grotto wasn't physically dangerous—unless you counted the couple of badly behaved children who had kicked him in the shins—but it all went to prove she didn't have to live for ever in that protective bubble she had created around herself. Doing something spontaneous caused her anxiety, but he had seen how much she'd enjoyed it tonight and when they had gone ice-skating. Not to mention their reckless non-relationship. At heart, Sophie was an adventurous spirit too. She just didn't know it yet.

'Are you ready to go?' When he walked back into the main hall the stallholders were packing up what was left of their stock. Sophie had apparently been buying in his absence, carrying a bag he hadn't noticed before.

'Ready when you are.' She took a grey chunky knit scarf out from the bag and tied it around his neck.

'For me?'

'Yeah, I know it's a cop-out since I didn't make it myself, but I thought we should keep the tradition going.' She was talking about the home-made gifts they used to exchange at Christmas. His had tended to be something to make her laugh, while Sophie had always put a lot of thought into making something special. He still had one or two.

'Christmas is weeks away yet.'

'I know, but we might not be together by then.'

He was about to ask why when he remembered the deal they had made. Time had got away from him since he and Sophie had hooked up and for once he wasn't looking for an escape route.

'It's the nature of my work, I'm afraid.'

'I know, there's always something more exciting around the corner.'

'Exactly.'

Sophie had hit the nail on the head, but he could see she wasn't thrilled about it. With his medical training, there were always new opportunities available to him. He'd worked as ambulance crew before, an exciting, unpredictable job which he had enjoyed. However, the chance of jumping out of helicopters for a living had been too perfect to walk away from. He didn't know what the future held for him, but he knew Carey Cove wasn't part of it. There were too many memories here for him. Especially the more recent ones he had made with Sophie.

He would never find anyone like her again, but settling down wasn't on the cards for him. Seeing her interact with the children tonight, it was easy to see she wanted to be part of one of those happy families who had come through the door. Roman couldn't imagine being a parent or a husband, having to change who he was to fit into either role. His mother and father had shown him that anything less than what people expected from him was unacceptable. Sophie needed someone safe, and that definitely wasn't Roman. If she didn't ask him for more than

he could give her they could keep pretending otherwise for a little while longer.

They walked towards Sophie's place in silence. The earlier frisson between them had
dissipated and she had become withdrawn.
He knew it was because of what he had said
about looking for the next thing to claim his
attention. That wasn't directed at her, but she
was going to have to get used to the idea of
him moving on. It was in the terms and conditions of their agreement.

Sophie suddenly called out and she gripped
hold of Roman's arm. 'Whoa. The ground's
starting to get icy. I should have worn my
skates to get home.'

Roman grabbed her tight and ushered her
away from the icy pavement. 'We should
walk on the grass. Less chance of breaking a leg.'

As he had done on the ice rink, he held
her hand as they picked their steps carefully,
ready to catch her if she fell.

'You couldn't have got us a ride home in
the helicopter?' she joked as her foot slipped
on a patch of crispy white grass and she lost
her balance.

He jerked her back and wrapped an arm
around her waist to keep her anchored. 'If I

thought for one second you would have got on board I would have.'

'Excuses, excuses.'

Roman knew she was still prickly about his earlier comment and he was glad they had this time walking home for him to try and win her over. He wanted them to enjoy whatever time they did have together.

'If you're keen, I'll put in a word and see if I can get you in for some training.' He called her bluff, knowing she would never agree to it.

'Okay, then.'

'Fine,' he retorted, convinced it was only irritation spurring her bravado.

As they lapsed back into a painful silence, with only the sound of the grass crunching beneath their feet, a car came skidding around the bend, headlights blindingly bright.

'Look out!' Desperate to keep Sophie out of the path of the vehicle now sliding across the road and onto the grass verge where they were walking, he pushed her away. If these were his last moments on earth, he wanted to do something to show her how much he cared for her.

It took a moment for Sophie to realise what had happened. The last thing she'd seen were car headlights, followed by the frantic sound of a horn and brakes screeching. She was sore, cold and lying in a ditch, but she was alive. Roman had pushed her out of the way. Roman! He was nowhere to be seen.

Her head was spinning, her stomach lurching at the thought of what could have happened to him.

'Roman!'

'Sophie? Where are you?' The sound of his voice made her want to cry with blessed relief that she hadn't lost him.

'Here!' She waved her hands over her head, hoping he could see above the ditch she had apparently rolled down.

Roman appeared above her and held out his hand towards her. 'Thank goodness you're all right. I'm sorry if I was too rough, but all I could think about was getting you away from danger.'

He helped her up the steep bank and Sophie climbed it in a zombie-like state. She was trying to process what had happened, including that his first thought had been for her. Either of them could have been seriously injured or killed, through no fault of their own. They had been walking on the grass to prevent an accident, and it brought it home to her that, no matter the steps she took to stay safe, there were always outside factors she had no control over. She could wrap herself in cotton wool for the rest of her life, but ultimately she had no real control over her own fate. It made her wonder how much she had been denying herself unnecessarily over the years. Especially when taking a risk had led to so much pleasure with Roman these past days. Although she was never going to be a daredevil like him, perhaps she should start living the life her mother and father had never got to have.

'I'm so glad you're okay.' When she reached the top of the grassy slope she threw her arms around Roman and hugged him tight, afraid to ever let go. She knew in that moment it would break her heart to lose him a second time. As much as she'd tried not to, she could no longer continue to deny that she was in love with Roman as much as ever.

He was in her every waking thought, as well as the raunchier ones she had in her sleep. She'd felt more alive in the few days she'd had with him than this past decade without him. They were still good together, making each other laugh and enjoying one another's company, but now as adults there was so much more to their relationship. Even if they were both afraid to call it such. The passion which flared to life every time they came into contact was like nothing else she had ever experienced before and, overall, having Roman back in her life again made it so much more fulfilling. She didn't want to lose him tonight, or ever. With only a limited time together, Sophie wondered how she could convince him to take the ultimate risk and stay indefinitely in Carey Cove. Give them a chance to explore their relationship further.

'I'm fine, but the driver's hurt. We need to help him.'

Despite her need to cling to Roman a while longer, she heard the urgency and concern for the driver in his voice and let go.

'What happened?'

'I think he skidded on the black ice and lost control of the car. It crashed into the trees back there.' Roman led her back to the scene of the accident and she realised just how far she had rolled. Thanks to him, she'd been kept out of harm's way, and thankfully he had too. She didn't know what she would have done if anything had happened to him. The young driver hadn't been so lucky. The front of the car was practically wrapped around the trunk of the tree, clearly having hit it at speed. The blinking headlights and ticking engine made the otherwise quiet scene foreboding.

While Roman wrenched the car door open to assess the driver's injuries he was able to tell her that the young man was unconscious and unresponsive but still breathing. Sophie made the call for an ambulance, despite her own shaken nerves. Once she had passed on the details of the accident and the driver's non-responsive state, she went to assist Roman. It was then she saw the smashed windscreen, streaked with blood, and the large gash on the young man's forehead.

'Should we move him?' Although he had been wearing his seatbelt, with a head or neck injury it would be risky to move the patient in case of exacerbating the injury.

'Normally I would wait for the emergency services to get here but there's smoke coming from the engine. I'm concerned in case the car catches fire, and in this case I think it's more important to get him to safety.'

'Whatever you think is best.' Since Roman had more experience dealing with road traffic accidents, she was happy to follow his lead. She trusted he knew what he was doing, just as he had trusted her judgement when it came to her patient's unexpected premature labour.

He managed to get the driver out and dragged him to a safe distance away from the car.

'He's not breathing. I think he's swallowed his tongue,' Roman told her, kneeling beside the unconscious man.

Sophie immediately took up position on the other side of the prostrate body to help. Although actually swallowing your tongue was impossible, it was the term used when the relaxed tongue muscle fell back to close the airway. Not unusual in circumstances where the patient was unconscious due to a blow to the head.

Roman supported the man's head and gently raised his jaw to open the airway, the movement forcing the tongue forward to unblock the airway. He listened for signs of breathing and checked his pulse. When Sophie saw the relief on his face she felt it too, knowing he had saved another life.

'He's breathing but we need to get him into the recovery position.'

Sophie extended the man's arm at a right angle to his body with the palm of his hand facing upward. She reached across for his other arm and brought it over, so the back of his hand was resting on the cheek closest to her. Roman set the man's knee at a right angle and rolled him over towards Sophie, his head supported by his bent arm. Roman tilted the chin up and made sure his airways remained clear and Sophie covered him with her coat to keep him warm. It was only then she and Roman were able to sit back and ruminate over what had happened. She didn't care that her backside was cold on the hard icy ground because she knew her shaky legs wouldn't hold her up.

'Thanks for saving me, Roman. I'm sure he'll thank you too when he's able to.' It was a feeble attempt at humour, but it did raise a smile from her companion.

'It was pure instinct. I just knew I had to get you somewhere safe.'

There was nothing she could say to that which wouldn't make her cry, so she simply shuffled over to sit beside him. Roman took his jacket off and wrapped it around their shoulders. Sophie tucked her head under his arm and cuddled into his warmth. It was all she needed to make her feel safe again, and that was the way the paramedics found them a few minutes later.

By the time they made it back to the cottage they were so cold and weary Roman insisted on heating some more mulled wine for them as a nightcap.

'To prevent shock,' he insisted.

It did go some way to warming her up again, but exhaustion had set into her very bones as they made their way to bed.

'I'm so tired I can't even be bothered to undress,' she said with a yawn, sitting on the end of the bed.

'That's because you've just been involved in a traumatic accident.' He came to kneel at her feet and began to undo her boots for her.

'So have you.' He'd been much closer to the accident and saved a life so she shouldn't really be the one complaining.

'Yeah, but I deal with these things a lot more often than you do. I can't say it doesn't affect me, but it will have been a bigger shock to your system than mine. Now lie back.'

'Sorry, I'm too tired, Roman.' As much as the wanting him never left her, she simply didn't have the energy for their enthusiastic lovemaking after everything they had gone through tonight.

He tutted. 'I wasn't talking about that. I'm trying to take care of you. Now, lie back.'

She did as she was told this time and lay there, half dreaming, she thought, as he stripped off her clothes, leaving her in just her underwear. He pulled back the covers and climbed into bed beside her, apparently having undressed without her witnessing it.

'So tired,' she mumbled, her eyes already closing.

'Go to sleep. I'll keep you safe.' They were the last words she heard, secure in Roman's warm embrace as sleep finally claimed her.

CHAPTER SIX

LAST NIGHT HAD been unsettling for Roman in so many ways. The car accident in itself had been traumatic, but so had that split-second of seeing the car hurtling towards Sophie. He had always been the one taking risks, much to her annoyance, and he'd recently been encouraging her to do the same. However, that near miss made him want to envelop her in protective bubble wrap for the rest of her life. An impossible task, literally and figuratively. Due to the unfortunate loss of her parents, Sophie had apparently lived her entire life keeping 'safe'. Yet she had still been in the path of that vehicle travelling at high speed. If he hadn't been there… Roman shuddered. Now they had reconnected he couldn't imagine not having her in his life. A problem in itself.

Despite not having his eye on more thrilling job opportunities, Roman feared it would soon be time to move on. Two things were inevitable about his return here and they would make a permanent stay impossible. He was bound to see his parents, whether through accident or choice, and it was sure to end in a row to sever their relationship once and for all. There was no chance they had changed their opinion of him in all this time, when they hadn't made any attempt to make amends and he had lived quite happily without their constant disdain in the meantime. The other factor was Sophie. This had to end between them, but it wasn't something he was looking forward to. He also knew he couldn't keep seeing her after the split. The temptation would be too great to make it into something more, when they both knew they weren't compatible. They would only end up hurting each other. Though he wasn't in a hurry to leave just yet…

She was curled up into him now, trusting him to keep her safe as he had promised. The words had slipped involuntarily out of his mouth, a natural reaction to almost losing her. Sophie needed him tonight and he wanted to be with her, but it was a promise he couldn't keep for ever.

'I can hear the cogs whirring in your head,' she mumbled. Roman had been so caught up in his thoughts he hadn't noticed the change in her breathing, signalling her return to consciousness.

'A lot happened last night. I keep going over it in my head. I mean, I didn't expect to have you turn up as one of Santa's helpers. If I had known I would have given you some pointy ears and stripy stockings.' It was much easier to joke about the events before the accident than tell Sophie what was really on his mind.

She playfully tweaked his nipple and though the slight, brief pain was unexpected, he was not averse to it. 'The idea of that would give anyone reason to be awake at this time of the morning.'

He kissed the top of her head. 'Even when you save a life it doesn't stop you going over what happened. I'm sure you know that.'

Although they were in different areas of medicine, Sophie was bound to have experienced her fair share of death and tragedy. Last night notwithstanding. It had the effect of making you evaluate your own life. He was certainly contemplating his future and how difficult it was going to be without Sophie in it. Yet the alternative seemed a step too far, even for a risk-taker like him.

She sat up. 'Usually I would be awake all

night, overthinking what happened, or could have happened, or what I should have done differently. I think I was too exhausted last night. It was nice having someone here to take my mind off things. For once, I wasn't going through it alone.'

Her words ought to have been enough to see him scrambling to get away and make the break. Instead, they simply made him want to cuddle her closer and lie here for ever if it brought her some peace. He owed her that much after years of her believing he had rejected her, that she was the one with the personality flaws instead of him. The idea of spending a day or more in bed with her was also appealing on a base level. Not only did it mean they wouldn't have to face reality for a while longer, but they could take their time getting to know each other's bodies all over again.

'I'm glad you're okay.' He dipped his head and kissed her.

'Thank you for saving me.' Sophie kissed him back.

'Any time.'

She snuggled back down against his chest. 'Do you…do you think we could keep this thing going for a while? I mean, we haven't killed each other yet and as far as I can tell we're enjoying each other's company...'

Roman's heart just about stopped. This was it. The moment when she had to go and spoil things by expecting too much from him. He closed his eyes and braced himself for the breakup speech he hadn't had the courage to say the last time he'd left her.

'Soph—'

'We may as well see Christmas through together. There's no point in both being alone on the day. No pressure, but we could have Christmas dinner here if neither of us are working. You'll want to go to the Guise Festival too. Everyone wears masks and costumes and there's a dance on the village green...' She was rambling, a habit she had when she was nervous, and he supposed it was because the idea was breaking all the rules of their arrangement. It made little difference when they'd already strayed away from the bedroom into almost dating territory, ice-skating and visiting the local fairs together.

He let out a heavy breath, thankful this didn't have to come to an end just yet. There was nothing appealing about spending the nights alone in his rented flat, never mind spending Christmas there too. At least there was a final date, so they knew the time frame they had to stick to—a Christmas Countdown he was both looking forward to and dreading at the same time.

'Is that what you want?'

'If that's what you want?'

They dodged around making the commitment, which was sufficient evidence for him to believe they could indulge themselves over the season without causing serious harm. This was simply a time extension to make the most of this thing between them before they went their separate ways.

'Just for Christmas?'

'Well, just for the sex,' she teased, running a fingertip across his chest.

'In that case, what are we doing wasting time talking?' He rolled Sophie over onto her back, her squeal of surprise soon turning to moans of pleasure as he stripped away her underwear and used his mouth to tend to all of her erogenous zones, worshipping her naked body with his searching lips and teasing tongue.

As long as he and Sophie both knew where they stood, Roman saw no reason why they couldn't continue their fling for now. They both deserved to have a little fun and lay a few ghosts to rest in the process. It was closure, not the start of something new and dangerous. He hoped.

Sophie had finished her last appointment of the day with her patient in Hodden village. Driving home, the sight of the Callahans' grand house on the hill caught her eye. She drove past it several times a week and never gave it a second thought. Despite it being Roman's childhood home, she didn't associate him with the place, probably because he had never really talked about it until the other night. Now all she could think about was how unhappy he must have been there, and how he was still avoiding the place.

When she came to the junction in the road where she should have turned off to head back to the cottage, she found herself driving into the large winding road up to the house instead.

She and Roman had had a breakthrough last night. Not only had he admitted how afraid he had been of losing her, to her surprise he had agreed to move the deadline of their liaison until after Christmas. With every moment she got to spend with him, she found herself wanting more. They were good together and, unless something drastic happened to change that, she wanted Roman in her life for as long as possible. Not only were they having the most incredible time in bed together, but he was broadening her horizons elsewhere too. She was beginning to see she couldn't keep herself locked away for ever. There was a world out there to explore, which didn't necessarily mean dangling on the end of a rope or jumping out of a helicopter. It simply meant putting herself out there, and she had certainly done that by asking him to stick around for a while longer.

There was one cloud on the horizon which might force him to leave again, and Sophie wanted to take steps to prevent that from happening. If they had a chance as a couple she didn't want his parents spoiling things a second time. A truce with his parents might encourage him to stay longer and think of a future with her.

She drew up to the house and managed to slip through the electric gates slowly closing after the car in front. Roman's parents, she presumed, seeing the family resemblance as they got out of their vehicle to glare at her. Although their features were sharper, and their mouths already tight with disapproval at her.

'Can we help you?' Mr Callahan asked,

his gruff demeanour already making her regret her decision to try and act as mediator between them and their son.

'I'm not sure if you remember me, Mr and Mrs Callahan. My name is Sophie French, I'm a friend of your son, Roman.' They would have no reason to know her since they had never been introduced, but she was counting on Roman having mentioned her at some point when they were growing up.

'Wait. Are you the girl he used to spend so much time with when he was young?' Mrs Callahan enquired, recognition clearly sparked by the mention of her name. Roman must have talked about her at home and the thought gave her a warm feeling inside, which was much needed at present.

'Roman and I were friends, yes.' They had gone long past that now, but these people didn't need to know that, even if she'd thought they had the slightest interest in their relationship.

'Well, we don't know where he is. He left here ten years ago in a fit of pique and we haven't heard from him since.' Mrs Callahan tilted her fine tapered nose into the air, clearly claiming the upper hand in the matter.

'I think it was more than a fit of pique,'

she muttered, aware of how great the decision to go must have been for Roman. He hadn't left behind everything he knew because he was having a teenage tantrum. It had been brave of him to follow his dream against his parents' wishes.

'Whatever it is you want from us, we can't help you.' Mrs Callahan locked the car and turned to go into the house, taking her husband's arm and leading him away too. Conversation over as far as they were concerned, but Sophie wasn't going without saying her piece. She owed it to Roman to try and get his family back for him before it was too late. Thinking about how lonely it must be for him, not having loved ones around, was too much for her to bear.

She had to move quickly to catch up with them before they disappeared inside the grand entrance.

'You misunderstand. I don't want anything from you. I simply wanted to let you know he's back, in Carey Cove. There might be a chance of reconciling if you could just sit down and talk with him.'

Mr and Mrs Callahan slowly turned to look at her. 'He's here?'

Sophie nodded. 'It was a surprise to me too, but he's doing really well. He's a paramedic with the emergency helicopter crew. You've probably seen it about. He's very brave, rescuing those in need of emergency medical help nearby.'

While she was singing Roman's praises Mrs Callahan was rolling her icy blue eyes. 'Still messing about and not taking life seriously, you mean. That boy will never grow up.'

Sophie couldn't understand what she was hearing. They had a virtual stranger telling them their son put his life in jeopardy every day to rescue those in distress and they were accusing him of acting the fool. If these had been her parents she would have been keen to walk away from the toxic atmosphere herself.

'I don't think you understand—'

'No, I don't think *you* understand, Ms French. We offered our son an enviable, lucrative position in our company. He would have been set for life, but he threw it back in our faces and went back to school rather than grow up and face his responsibilities.' Mr Callahan was becoming agitated now as he vented his disappointment in his son's choices, a bizarre reaction to a man who only wanted to help people. A concept, Sophie assumed, his family couldn't comprehend against their own selfish wants.

She thought she would take one last shot to get them to see what a wonderful man Roman was before they, and she, lost him for good. 'Roman is a good man. He cares deeply for other people and he has saved countless lives over the years. You should be proud of him. I think if you would sit down and talk with him you would realise you were wrong about him.'

Mr Callahan's face was as dark and foreboding as thunder. 'Please do not presume to know anything about us or our family. Roman chose to walk away from his family and good career prospects and you think you can come here and tell us we were the ones in the wrong? We have nothing to say to you or Roman. Come along, Penny. We don't have to listen to this.'

'Roman is a good man,' she insisted as they turned their backs on her again, refusing to hear it. They walked inside and slammed the door on her.

Sophie shuddered and pulled her cardigan closer around her shoulders. She had come uninvited, but in her opinion they were the ones being rude when they wouldn't even invite her inside to hear what she had to say.

It was no wonder Roman thought he had no other choice but to walk away, and why he refused to even see them. She could only imagine the way they'd talked to him when they had been so rude to her, a stranger on their doorstep.

All of a sudden she was infused with rage on his behalf. They had no right to look down their noses at her or Roman simply because they had more money and didn't appreciate or respect the medical profession as much as they should. Normally she wouldn't interfere in anyone's personal matters but Roman was different. She couldn't bear to hear his own parents make disparaging remarks about their wonderful son.

Without taking time to take a deep breath and count to ten, Sophie marched straight up to the door and banged on it. Roman deserved more from his family and if he wouldn't say it, she would.

There was no answer from inside, but she wasn't about to walk away without saying her piece. She kept hammering on the door until it was wrenched open again and she was faced with the red-faced Mr Callahan.

'We have said all we are going to say on the subject of our son.' It was plain to see nothing Roman did would ever be enough in their eyes unless he submitted to their wishes and joined the family business. Controlling, manipulative behaviour which no longer had a hold on Roman, and that was probably what drove them mad.

'Well, I haven't.' She wedged her foot in the door, holding it open until she said what she had come here to say. Okay, so it wasn't going to end up in a tearful family reunion after all, but they would hear her out.

'Your egos might not let you be proud of your son but, let me tell you, he is the most courageous man I have ever met. He puts his own life on the line day in and day out to help others in need. To me that means so much more about a man who could have happily sat behind a desk and accepted a big, fat pay cheque at the end of every month. It was his dream to make a difference to other people's lives, not just his own. You don't know what you have missed out on with your petty grievance that he wouldn't fall into line and join the family business. He has his own mind and, yes, he takes more risks than most sane people, but that is what makes Roman the man he is.' It was on the tip of her tongue to say he was the man she loved, but that was probably obvious without saying the words. Why else would she be here defending him to his parents?

The effort of trying to get them to open their hearts and minds to the wonderful man he was, and getting no response, brought tears to her eyes and with a grunt of frustration she had to admit defeat. Sophie withdrew her foot from the doorjamb and made her way back to the car. She didn't know how Roman would react to the news that she had come here, or that it had been entirely futile. Indeed, it remained to be seen if she would even tell him. He might not be best pleased that she had done so without consulting him first.

The visit did settle one question in her mind though: they would never reconcile with Roman. It was obvious nothing he said or did would ever be enough for them to let him back into their lives, even if he wanted that. The fact that they wouldn't even listen to anything good she had to say about him was proof of their continued—and, in her opinion, misdirected—disdain. Whether Roman would appreciate her attempt to end their estrangement or treat her involvement in the matter as brusquely as his parents remained to be seen.

In future she wouldn't interfere in Roman's issues with his parents or judge him for wanting to keep his distance from them. At least her family had loved her, even if her parents had spent most of their lives chasing adventure. Just like Roman. They might not have been in her life as much as she'd wanted but they had never bullied her into doing what they'd wanted. She had put the pressure on herself to be more like them, believing she had to change to suit them. Deep down, she knew they'd loved her, even if it had been from a distance at times. They'd never come home without a present for her and tales to tell her at bedtime. She couldn't recreate that kind of parental love for herself or Roman, no matter how hard she tried.

It was difficult to comprehend how the Callahans couldn't love their own son when she couldn't stop herself falling deeper for him every day. They had agreed to keep their casual arrangement going until Christmas, but in her heart she knew that would never be enough for her. After meeting Roman's parents it didn't seem fair to keep him here solely for her benefit, where he was reminded of the pain of his childhood every day.

As she drove home her heart was heavy with the knowledge that the fantasy was coming to an end. For the second time, Roman would be leaving her and there was nothing she could do about it.

Regardless of how weary he was, Roman couldn't wait to get back and see Sophie. They both had very demanding jobs, but they had fallen into an after-work routine of dinner together and chilling out in front of the television for a few hours before going to bed. Other than collecting clean clothes and showering, he had spent little time in his own apartment since meeting Sophie again two weeks ago. He was getting too comfortable with the situation, but he couldn't find it in him to disrupt what they had together. It was a long time since he had felt so enamoured by someone and cherished in return. An intoxicating state of affairs for someone who was not used to the comfort of a loving home to come back to. If he had been the settling-down type he would have happily moved in with Sophie if she'd asked him but, as it was, he was content to take things day by day. The alternative was to move on, and he wasn't ready to do that just yet.

He was almost sprinting up to her front door in his haste to see her. As he made his way up the path she threw open the door, as though she had been waiting for him with equal impatience. Roman launched himself at her and Sophie flung her arms around his neck. They were a hot tangle of mouths and limbs as he backed her into the hallway.

He wondered if it would always be like this or if the novelty would eventually wear off. It was hard to believe he would ever tire of the taste of Sophie on his lips, or the feel of her in his arms. Certainly his body reacted to her as if he was seeing her for the first time whenever they met up at the end of the working day.

'Hello to you too,' Sophie panted when they eventually came up for air between kisses.

'I missed you,' he admitted, even though it would have been obvious from his enthusiastic greeting.

'You only saw me this morning,' she said, laughing, though she was clinging to him as though they'd been parted for months too.

'It's been a long day.' One shift including a woman who had come off her horse and broken her back and a climber who had fallen and knocked himself unconscious had made the day seem never-ending. The thought of being here with Sophie was the thing that had got him through the danger and drama.

'Speaking of which… I have something to tell you—'

'Later. Right now, all I want is to take you to bed and forget everything else that happened today.' He wanted to lose himself with her, in her, and ignore the warnings his inner voice was shouting at him that he was getting too involved with Sophie. That she was such a big part of his life again that walking away was going to be as painful as it had been first time around. If not more. Even if he didn't leave now, he was sure the urge to keep moving would come eventually. That was who he was, a nomad who did better on his own than he ever did with anyone else. He was sure this contentment he had with Sophie could only ever be fleeting. That panic would inevitably set in when sharing his life with someone made him feel trapped, as though he was compromising who he was for their happiness. He much preferred dancing to the beat of his own drum. Usually. For now he was having way too much fun with Sophie to worry about the future.

'But—' She made a half-hearted attempt to put the brakes on as he backed her towards the bedroom, but Roman had no desire to talk about work or anything else which might bring reality in to spoil everything.

'But what? Is there something else you'd rather be doing than this?' He kissed her neck at the spot he knew made her go weak at the knees and began unbuttoning her tunic.

'N-no,' she gasped. He could feel the frantic beat of her pulse under his lips and knew she needed this as much as he did.

'Right answer.' He slipped her clothes off and divested himself of his own, leaving a trail down the hall towards the bedroom. This was only supposed to be about sex and if they kept it that way, free of emotions and feelings, they could keep seeing each other without fear of repercussions.

Sophie knew she was being a coward. She needed to tell Roman everything that had happened today, but admitting she had gone to his parents behind his back was sure to anger him. Perhaps it was selfish of her to go along with this, knowing it was likely for the last time, but she needed it—she needed Roman.

He was making it impossible for her to think or even begin to recount the events of the day anyway when he was so clearly intent on seducing her. With his hands, his mouth, his tongue…

Sophie didn't know how she came to be on the bed, so lost to the sensations he was creating within her. They were both naked, Roman's body a perfect study of masculinity in the moonlight. The silver glow of the night highlighted every curve of muscle and delineated plane of his torso. She smoothed her hand over his rippled abdomen, marvelling at his beauty and hoping to capture the sight and feel of him in her mind for ever.

His kisses were passionate, but for her they held a certain pathos because she knew this was all going to end too soon. Their lovemaking was slow and intense, like a lingering last goodbye. Her climax came with a cry of anguish mixed in with the temporary euphoria, knowing she would never have this again. No one else could ever make her feel the way Roman did.

Before they could even catch their breath properly, the guilt poured out of her about what she had done.

'I have something to tell you, Roman.'

He rolled over onto his side, head propped on his bent arm, listening intently to what she had to say.

Sophie gulped. She tried to think of a way to ease gently towards recounting the events but there were no words to soften the harsh reality of what had happened.

'I hope you're not about to tell me you're married and I'm going to have your estranged husband after me.' The shine of his smile in the darkness melted her heart, no less because she knew it would soon disappear.

'No, I'm not married. I… I went to see your parents today.'

She braced herself for fireworks, but the ensuing silence was somehow even worse.

'Did you hear me, Roman? I spoke to your mum and dad.'

'I heard you. I'm trying to figure out why you would do that.'

Sophie sat up, clutching the sheets to her like a security blanket as she replayed the whole terrible scene in her mind. 'I thought if I could get them to talk to you there might be a chance you would stay for good.'

'That wasn't the deal.' The scowl didn't have as much aesthetic appeal as the short-lived smile.

'I know… I just… I thought since they were the reason you left the last time, if you could patch things up we might have the chance of a future together.' She was taking the biggest risk of her life by admitting that was what she wanted when Roman had told her that was not possible, but she was going to lose him anyway if they kept to their Christmas schedule. When there was a tiny chance of him wanting the same thing, Sophie was willing to take the gamble.

'And? What did they have to say?'

This was the hard part. Once she told him that she had resolved nothing, probably only made matters worse, there would be no reason for him to want to stick around, but she owed it to him to tell the truth.

'They didn't want to talk about you or listen to anything I had to say.' The cruelty of it made her want to weep for the young Roman, who'd had to live with that vitriol his whole life. Ten minutes in their company had been sufficient to understand what a toxic home environment he had grown up in and why he'd spent so much time with her and her gran.

Roman's mirthless laugh sent chills across her skin. 'Don't say I didn't warn you.'

'I know.' She'd spent the rest of the afternoon and evening unsuccessfully trying to come up with an explanation for Roman which would not paint her as the interfering busybody she was.

He scrubbed his hands over his face and scalp, almost tearing his hair out at her actions, and Sophie was chastised all over again.

'I'm sorry. I was trying to help.'

'No, you were trying to manipulate things to suit you, Sophie. I told you I didn't want to speak to them. Warned you that I'm not relationship material, yet you believe you can change the way I think. That's the type of behaviour I really cannot live with. It's why I left in the first place.' He climbed out of bed and began pulling on his clothes with a different urgency than when he'd torn them off. Now he couldn't wait to get away from her.

'Is it so wrong of me to want more time with you?'

'Yes. Everybody wants something more from me, then they're disappointed when I'm found wanting. You knew who I was when you agreed to this. It's not fair to expect me to fit into the mould of the man you should be with. That's not me, Sophie.'

But she wanted it to be and that was the whole problem.

'So you're leaving me?'

Just like her mum and dad and her gran.

She wasn't enough to keep Roman with her here either.

'That was always the plan. It wasn't me who changed it. I'm sorry, Sophie, but this is going to have to be the end.'

'It doesn't have to be. I messed up. I'm sorry. Don't let one mistake ruin what we could have here.'

Roman pulled his sweater over his head and perched on the side of the bed. 'It's not just about you going to see my parents, don't you see? Your reason for doing so was because you thought it would change my mind about what I want. Who I am. It's simply opened my eyes to our differences. You need someone who wants to settle down, who will give you the security you crave. We both know that's not me. I made that clear from the start.'

'I know, but—'

'No buts, no exceptions. There's no point delaying the inevitable when it'll just cause more hurt.'

Too late, she thought. Her heart was breaking, slowly and painfully, with his every word. If she thought it would make any difference she would drop to her knees and beg him to stay, but he had that same look on his face as he had the last time he'd walked away from her. His mind was made up and she had no say in the matter.

'You're leaving me.' It was a statement of fact in her attempt to believe it was actually happening. Her life had been so full these past weeks, so consumed was she with Roman and being with him. Now she didn't know how she was going to carry on without him. How could she possibly go back to her old life when she'd had a taste of a better one with Roman in it?

'I was always going to. I thought you understood that.'

She nodded. He was right, of course. She had agreed to this fling on the basis that it would never be anything serious. That hadn't stopped her yearning for more. It was her own fault she was hurting so much now. Roman didn't owe her anything. He simply didn't love her as much as she loved him and never had.

She was totally exposed, physically and emotionally, and when he moved towards the door she didn't follow. There was no certainty her legs would carry her when her whole body had gone into shock at her loss. Even the tears wouldn't come, though they were there hiding and waiting until she accepted it was over for ever.

'Goodbye, Sophie, and thank you for everything.' He hesitated for a moment in the doorway, perhaps waiting for her to repeat the sentiment and provide him with a guilt-free getaway. She couldn't bring herself to do it. To make it final.

When she was not forthcoming with the response he desired, Roman gave her a half smile she liked to imagine was full of regret for everything he was throwing away, turned and walked away.

She watched him until he had disappeared out of her sight and her life, not knowing how she was going to recover a second time from a broken heart.

CHAPTER SEVEN

SOPHIE LAY IN the dark for some time, replaying everything that had happened between her and Roman, the good and the bad, until she could bear the memories no longer. It was late but she knew sleep would not be forthcoming and needed something to take her mind off her loss. She left her discarded clothes lying on the floor, the memory of Roman taking them off in a frenzy of desire too much for her to face.

A run, that was what she needed. She donned her running gear and added a few extra layers to protect her from the cold. Scarf, gloves and trainers on, she was ready to escape the ghost of Roman, trapped for ever in the cottage with her.

It was pitch-black outside, save for the stars and moon shining above, and she could see her puffs of breath hanging in the air as she ran but the conditions didn't faze her.

The cold would revive her flagging spirit; the dark would hide the tears sure to fall. She hadn't run the whole time she and Roman had been together, preferring to get her exercise in the bedroom. Now she had no choice.

Sophie ran along the coast road, the thunder of the sea doing little to block out the voice in her head grieving the death of her relationship with Roman, even if it had been all in her head.

She pounded the tarmac until her lungs were burning and her legs were jelly. Curse Roman Callahan for coming back here and stirring up her feelings, only to run out on her again. She could happily have spent the rest of her life in ignorance of the fantastic sex life she could have or how much more her very existence would be with Roman in it. Now she would spend the rest of her days mourning it all.

Eventually she had to stop for a break, bending over double and gasping for air. It was then she noticed the safety barrier which ran alongside the road was damaged. Something had crashed straight through it, leaving bits of glass and debris glinting on the ground.

Sophie peered over the edge of the cliff,

the long way down and the vicious waves crashing below making her dizzy.

'Hello! Is there anyone down there?' she shouted into the night. It was difficult to see anything, but she thought she saw a wisp of smoke and the flash of something on the ledge halfway down.

A faint, 'Help!' drifted up to her on the wind.

Sophie's heart was hammering with fear and trepidation. Someone was down there, and she was the only one around to provide assistance. She remembered her phone and pulled it out of her pocket, hoping the light would help her spot whoever it was in trouble. As she squinted into the shaft of light she could just make out the car which had thankfully landed right side up, but was now resting precariously on a rocky shelf halfway down the cliffside. The small yellow hatchback was instantly recognisable to her and it made her stomach tighten into a knot of anxiety. It belonged to one of her patients.

'Kirstie? Is that you?'

The small figure bent over at the side of the car straightened up and waved. 'Yes. Can you send help?'

'It's Sophie French. Are you hurt?' She wanted to know what she was dealing with so she could pass it on to the emergency services and better prepare them for her rescue.

'Just a bit shaken… Argh!' Kirstie's assurance that she was fine was belied by the loud groan which followed.

'Kirstie?'

The groaning went on for a few more seconds and Sophie grew concerned that she had hurt herself and was no longer able to communicate. She dialled for the emergency services, knowing that there was only one team who could possibly get down there to help her.

'I'm having contractions and I think my waters broke.' The voice came from the darkness just as Sophie was relaying directions to the operator, making the rescue more urgent than ever.

'Oh, and please get here as soon as possible. The lady is in labour.'

'Roman?'

'Hello, Mother.'

Roman was almost as shocked as she was to find him pitched up on the doorstep of the family home. It was the argument with Sophie which had finally prompted him to confront them. He'd burned his bridges where she was concerned so he might as well raze the whole of Carey Cove to the ground while he was here. There was no way he could ever come back now. Without Sophie, there was nothing for him here. They'd had closure of a kind, even if he had so much more to regret when he thought of her. So many more memories to torture him at night when he was in bed alone, because if he couldn't make it work with the only woman he'd ever loved he couldn't make it work with anyone else. Now it was time to get closure on the rest of his life at Carey Cove.

He'd been avoiding this confrontation for too long, afraid of what they would say and of how they might make him feel, but nothing could make him feel any worse about himself today.

'Can I come in?' She hadn't slammed the door shut in his face already, which he was taking as a good sign and pushed a little more.

Although his mother didn't make a formal invitation, she did step aside to allow him entrance.

'Your father is in the lounge.' It was difficult to tell if it was an instruction or warning but that was where he headed, his heart pumping in time with his fast steps. This conversation was long overdue, though the thought of saying what he needed to remained a daunting prospect.

'What are you doing here?' The first unwelcoming words out of his father's mouth were not surprising but they were still capable of wounding, with the suggestion he didn't belong in the family home. Roman had never expected a happy reunion but there was a part of him hoping his parents might have mellowed over the years.

With Sophie having interfered, they at least knew he was in town and he would have expected it to prompt a conversation between his parents at least. If there had been one, obviously they hadn't revised their opinion of him.

What was he doing here? What had he hoped to achieve by coming here, other than another argument? Deep down he knew it wouldn't change anything, but Sophie had braved their wrath to say her piece and now it was his turn. He hadn't appreciated her trying to manipulate the situation to get him to stay but he did admire her courage in coming to speak to his parents when he had chickened out of doing it until now. They had both found courage in each other to brave the things they feared the most.

'I've been working locally and I thought it

was about time I paid a visit.' Although neither of his parents had invited him to take a seat, Roman plonked himself down into an armchair.

His father, who had been sitting with his feet up, was now standing, no doubt readying himself for a fight. His mother was hovering in the doorway, apparently reluctant to be in the midst of the imminent fray.

'It took you long enough.'

Roman knew his father wasn't claiming they would have expected him to come earlier but seizing the opportunity, as always, to have a dig at him. A good son—either of his brothers—would have made home their first stop. It didn't matter that they hadn't contacted him over the years, it was another chance to highlight Roman's many failings. Not that they needed to. His breakup with Sophie, his inability to commit to the woman he loved, already proved what a disappointment he was to everyone.

Nevertheless, Roman tried to ignore the jibe so he didn't get distracted from what he had come here to say.

'Well, I'm here now. Although not for long. I'm only on a temporary contract.'

'Yes, your friend Sophie mentioned you were working on a helicopter or something,' his mother butted in then to acknowledge their other unexpected visitor, who likely hadn't had a better reception than he had.

'I'm a paramedic on board the helicopter for medical emergencies.' Roman wanted them to know he wasn't simply messing about in the skies for fun, that his was a noble profession, even if it wasn't the one they had chosen for him.

'It's only temporary, though? Don't you think it's about time you got a proper job?' Now it was his mother's turn to disparage his accomplishments. He'd forgotten how they liked to tag team with their criticism. Although it was possible the comments were stinging so much more because there was some truth in what they were saying. He couldn't go on moving from one place to another for ever, never setting down roots. It was about time he found himself a permanent position and, though he enjoyed the work he was doing here, his wreck of a personal life made it impossible for him to stay. He was going to have to put more effort into finding a permanent position and finally settle somewhere. Once he had said his piece and probably seen his parents for the last time, he was hoping it would close the chapter of his life in Carey Cove for good and let him move on.

'I save lives every day. I wouldn't have thought there was a job much more admirable than that.' There was no point being coy about it when he was being forced to defend his job as a key health worker. Any normal family would be proud of him.

'There was a place right here at home for you,' his father grumbled, remaining unimpressed by his achievements.

'I know that, Dad. It's not like you didn't tell me every day of my damn life.' It was impossible not to bite back after years of repressing the hurt they had caused him. The best kind of therapy was probably to get it off his chest once and for all about the damage they had caused him growing up.

Except, before he had time to elaborate, his father had crossed the room to stand in front of him, red in the face and pointing a finger at him. 'We gave you everything and you threw it back in our faces.'

'Why can't you see it wasn't about you? It was about me.'

'You always made everything about you, Roman. You couldn't just fall into line like your brothers, it was one drama and tantrum after another.' Spittle was forming in the corners of his father's mouth as he let rip at Roman, but he had enough anger of his own to fuel retaliation.

'That's it, isn't it? You couldn't control me the way you do everyone else, so you made my life hell when I was growing up.'

'Roman! We only ever wanted the best for you,' his mother interjected as she came to join them in the room.

'No, you wanted what was best for you. Another slave with no will of his own who you could manipulate at will. You should have been proud you had a son who knew his own mind. What was so wrong about wanting to help sick people, for goodness' sake?'

'I worked my backside off to build my business, to give you kids a secure future, and you just threw it back in my face.' His father was so focused on the snub to his legacy that he wasn't listening to what Roman was saying.

'You have to see how it looked to us, Roman. Everything we gave you, everything we had planned for you just wasn't enough. Your brothers are happy in the family business and you, who wanted to go your own way, are still moving from one job to another. That doesn't sound like someone who is content with their choice. The two of you are both too stubborn to admit when you're wrong.' It was his mother who was trying to find some common ground between them but Roman knew she was fighting a lost cause when his father was waving a hand at her, dismissing everything she had to say.

'You never asked me what I wanted and if I dared to tell you I was shot down. You had no interest. I was supposed to shut up and do as I was told. I wasn't ungrateful, I was unhappy. Why do you think I spent so much time at Sophie's house when we were kids?'

'What went on in this house was none of anybody else's business.'

'Dad, you're focusing on the wrong details. Oh, this is pointless.' Admitting defeat, Roman got to his feet and prepared to leave. 'I just came to tell you what I was doing. I didn't expect you to approve, but don't worry, I won't be coming back any time soon.'

'Good. All you've succeeded in doing is upsetting your mother and me,' his father shouted at Roman's back, since he was already on his way out to the door.

Roman spun around with one last thing to get off his chest. 'Do you know why I don't stay in one place for too long, why I haven't settled down with a wife and kids? Because you made me feel as though I wasn't good enough for anyone. Perhaps if you had shown one iota of love towards me as a child things would have been different and I wouldn't be walking out on Sophie again.'

He hadn't meant to let that last comment slip out but in the heat of the moment it was her face which had flashed before his eyes. She was the biggest loss in his life, and he knew if he hadn't been so damaged by his relationship with his parents he would have been trying to fix things. He wouldn't have interpreted her attempt to talk to them as manipulative if he hadn't spent his whole life with his parents trying to control him.

'You never did take responsibility for anything, Roman. Was it any wonder we tried to give you a secure future when you seemed so determined to mess your life up? Don't blame your mother and me for your failed relationships. I'm sure you managed to mess those up all on your own, son.' Apparently having finished what he had to say, Roman's father went to sit in a chair but suddenly clutched his left arm and collapsed onto the floor.

His mother let out a scream.

'Dad?' Despite the bad blood between them, Roman immediately rushed to assist him.

The look of fear in his father's wide eyes was something he had never witnessed before and never wanted to see again. His skin was pale and clammy as Roman undid the top buttons of his shirt to loosen the fabric and help him breathe a bit easier.

'Dad? Can you hear me?'

He was unresponsive, his breathing and pulse weak.

'I think you're going into cardiac arrest but it's okay, I'm here. Mum, go and phone an ambulance.'

'Is he going to be okay, Roman?' his mother asked, already in tears.

'We need to get help as soon as possible. Now, please, do as I say.'

She rushed off, leaving Roman to apply chest compressions to try and keep the blood pumping around his father's body. Kneeling by his side, Roman leaned over and, with arms straight, fingers interlocked, he began pushing down onto his chest.

'The ambulance is on its way.' His mother came back into the room with the news he needed to hear.

'Come on, Dad. I know you're a stubborn

so-and-so. Come back.' He was doing all he could for now, but Roman still felt helpless as they waited for the paramedics to arrive. Despite everything which had taken place tonight, he knew if anything happened to his father he would never forgive himself. Just because they didn't see eye to eye, it didn't mean he didn't love him.

If his father didn't make it through this and they hadn't resolved their ill feeling, Roman knew it would haunt him for the rest of his days. He would agree to disagree with his parents on the subject of his choice of career if they could simply let him live his life without constant criticism.

Thankfully the ambulance turned up within minutes before guilt got the better of him that he had caused his father's heart attack by turning up here and he did something stupid like agree to work in the family firm after all.

Roman gave the paramedics the lowdown on what had happened. There was still no sign of life from his father, but he continued with CPR until they cut his clothes for the defibrillator they had brought with them.

They attached the pads and relieved him of his duty as the defibrillator took over. It delivered the first shock to try and get his heart back to a normal rhythm. When it was unsuccessful, the paramedic delivered some more chest compressions. After another shock his father opened his eyes and attempted to talk.

'Don't try to speak, Dad. You need all your strength. Let the paramedics look after you.' Roman took his father's hand and tried not to get in the way as the medics got ready to transfer him to the ambulance. His legs were so wobbly he was in danger of collapsing himself after the drama and subsequent relief of averting disaster.

'Thank goodness. I thought I'd lost you, Edward.' His mother was weeping beside him and he let go of his father's hand so she could take his place. Roman was sure he would prefer to see her face than his during his near-death experience.

They walked the stretcher out to the ambulance and his mother climbed into the back of the vehicle. Before he could follow, he was buzzed for a medical emergency. Checking his messages, he felt his mouth go dry and his stomach roll as he saw the details of a road traffic incident involving a midwife.

'Is that work?' his mother asked.

Roman nodded. 'It might be Sophie. We… er…had a row and there's been an accident…'

There was no way of knowing for sure if it was her but he couldn't take the chance in case something had happened to her. Except his father was on the way to the hospital after a heart attack too. He was torn about whether or not to get into the ambulance.

'Then go. You saved your father's life and if Sophie's in trouble she needs you.' With a quick and unexpected hug, his mother gave him her blessing. His throat constricted against the emotions bubbling up inside him at that simple sign of affection denied him so long. It was the acknowledgement he had waited for from his parents all of his life, that he had finally done something right and worthwhile.

It was the sort of pivotal moment he would have been running to Sophie to share. He could only hope he wasn't too late and there was still time to salvage a relationship with her as well.

'I'll be down to see you as soon as I can.' Roman closed one of the ambulance doors, with his father still in his line of sight. Lying on the stretcher, as pale as the white cotton sheet draped over him and attached to the machines monitoring his heart, he no longer looked like the intimidating adult who had cowed him throughout his childhood. Here, he was simply a frail old man fighting for his life and Roman actually felt sorry for him. It was a start to any idea of reconciliation that his emotions extended beyond anger and fear and he hoped, if his father's condition improved, they could find some way to mend bridges.

Just as he was closing the other door, his father sat up and pulled off his oxygen mask.

'Thanks, son,' he managed before he collapsed back down again.

This time Roman couldn't stop the sob which erupted from his throat. He had actually done something to make his parents appreciate the road he had taken. Perhaps he wasn't a waste of space after all and there might be something to stick around for, as long as Sophie was okay and was willing to forgive him.

Roman didn't know what could travel quicker than a helicopter but he wished he was in it. Considering the weather and time of year, road traffic accidents were unfortunately all too common. The location would make it tricky, but nothing they hadn't dealt with before. It was the possibility of Sophie being involved which terrified him. He knew he'd upset Sophie, yet he'd left her alone and now she might be lying hurt somewhere.

It had only been a matter of hours, but he already knew he'd made the biggest mistake of his life in leaving her again. She had been naked in bed and asking him to stay. Would it really have been so wrong to try and make things work? Yes, he'd let her down in the past, but she'd been willing to give him a second chance. And he'd been afraid of opening up his heart and sharing his life with anyone when he'd been so independent for so long. Sophie loved him, it showed in her every action and, though it scared the life out of him, Roman knew he loved her too. Now it might be too late to do anything about it.

'Are we nearly there?' he asked into his headset, poised to lower himself down the second they spotted whoever it was in trouble out there. If it was Sophie he would put his life on the line without a second thought to save her.

'You in a hurry to be somewhere else tonight, Callahan?'

'He must have a hot date.'

The other guys on the crew teased him with their usual banter. This was just another call to them and to deal with the stress and horror of the job they often used humour to defuse the tension. They weren't to know how shaken Roman was about this one, or how he might be personally involved. If they had they probably wouldn't have allowed him to go out on the call. Exactly why he hadn't informed them of a potential connection to the injured party. No matter how experienced the rest of the team was, he wasn't going to put Sophie's life in anyone's hands but his. That was where she belonged and the next time he had her there he wouldn't let her go. He prayed nothing had happened to her.

'I can see someone on top of the cliff.' A figure in a reflective top lit up under the helicopter's spotlights. As they came closer he could see it was Sophie and he almost collapsed with relief. Then he remembered there was still someone in trouble down there and steeled himself once more to run into the fray.

The reason he had taken this job was for this kind of adrenaline-pumping, life or death scenario that would never be boring. Although tonight he was regretting ever leaving Sophie's bed. He'd been stupid to think that would never be enough to satisfy them both when they had been perfectly happy these past days. Using the excuse that Sophie had been trying to manipulate him the way his parents had was nonsense and he knew it. It was a knee-jerk reaction to what she'd done. Going to talk to his parents, trying to reason with them so he would have reason to stay was something done out of love, and that was what had terrified him. Sophie was the only person who had ever loved him for who he was, way back when he was a wayward kid and again now, as an adult still scarred by his childhood.

'We'll put down in the field over there,' the pilot informed him, crushing any idea he had of abseiling down and grabbing hold of her for a windswept kiss. The job had to come first.

The second the chopper set down in the field Roman grabbed his medical equipment and climbing equipment for getting down to the patient and he and his colleague, Griff, ran towards where he had seen Sophie on the clifftop.

'Roman?' She seemed surprised to see him, but he was sure he could also see relief in her eyes. Or was that wishful thinking on his part?

'Hey, can you tell me what happened?' He had to resist getting personal for now and keep his focus on getting down that cliff-side without injuring himself or anyone else.

'I didn't see, but the car went through the barrier and came to rest on the ledge down there. I know the driver, Kirstie. I don't think she's injured but she is in labour. How on earth are you going to get her up here if she's about to give birth?'

'One step at a time. I need to get down to her and then we'll see how best to proceed.'

Sophie digested the information then stood a little straighter, her chin tilted up with a determination he knew too well. 'I'm coming down with you.'

It took a moment for Roman to realise what she was saying. 'No way. I don't have time to coax you down there and I'm not having you risking your life. I'll do this on my own.'

'It's not up for discussion. Kirstie is in labour. She's my patient and she needs me. Now, show me what I have to do.' Sophie asserted her position, regardless that this expedition went against every notion of keeping herself safe.

'She's right, Roman. If there are any complications you're going to need a qualified midwife down there. I'm sure the two of us can coach Sophie through everything she needs to know to get down there.' Griff offered his opinion, though Roman already knew what needed to be done. He simply wasn't happy about it.

Sophie was putting her patient first and facing all of her fears to do so. It only made Roman love her even more.

So many emotions were flowing around Sophie's body they were in danger of making her dizzy. Not a good omen if she was about to chuck herself over a cliff. She was afraid for Kirstie and the baby, for Roman and for herself. Seeing him again had brought a surge of relief tinged with sadness that he would never be hers again. As ever, it was the priority of her patient which won out.

'If you're sure, we'll get you kitted out with all the necessary safety equipment.' Roman waited, probably giving her a chance to change her mind when he knew how scared this sort of thing made her.

'I'm sure.' She trusted him to get her down safely, just as Kirstie would have faith in her doing her job and delivering her baby, regardless of the circumstances. They might still have time to get her to the hospital before the birth but at least if Sophie was there it might put Kirstie's mind at ease.

Roman and his colleague got her rigged out before he kitted himself out with the climbing gear. All the while he was shouting down to Kirstie, letting her know what was happening and that help was on the way. Sophie could only pray that she didn't get tangled, lose her nerve or plummet to the bottom of the cliff and end up needing to be rescued herself.

Roman tugged at her straps to make sure everything was secure and checked her safety helmet was on tight, even after Griff had already carried out the checks. 'Are you ready to do this?'

She gulped and nodded, though her very soul was shouting, *No!* There was never going to be a time when she was ready to launch herself off a cliff.

'Okay, you need to go to the edge and lean back.' He walked back with her to the end of the clifftop.

Apparently there was something more terrifying than mountain-climbing and that was doing it backwards in the dark. Although they had torches on their helmets and Griff was shining a light source down the cliff side, she really was going into the unknown, not able to see anything other than that directly in front of her. Perhaps that was a good thing when she could hear the wind whistling around her and the sea crashing down below. One wrong move and she could be plummeting to her death, just like her parents.

'I won't die, will I?' Roman had promised her once he would keep her safe and she needed that reassurance more than ever, regardless if he wanted her or not.

'Not if I can help it.' With the solid set of his jaw, Sophie was inclined to believe him and took a deep breath, preparing to take the biggest risk of her life.

'Just keep talking to me so I know I'm not doing this alone.' With Roman by her side she might be more inclined to think she could actually do this. It was hard to believe he did this on a regular basis as a job and she had nothing but admiration for him, even if she did think he was crazy. The world needed more crazy people to do jobs like this, risking their lives daily to save others.

'No problem. I'm here for you. Now, ease yourself over the edge and just walk back, feet against the cliff.'

It sounded so simple until she thought about something going wrong and instead of walking down the drop her feet might refuse to move and she'd go head first. Roman disappeared over the cliff but she knew he was waiting for her to follow. She didn't have time to overthink and panic when Kirstie was down below, in labour.

A few more deep breaths and she followed her companion, clinging tight to the rope she was dangling from.

'We can take this slow. Gently bounce against the cliff as you make your way down, feeding the guide rope through your hands.' Roman demonstrated a couple of steps, basically walking down the cliff at almost a ninety-degree angle, not bothered that there was only a rope stopping him from tumbling to his death.

Sophie concentrated her thoughts on her patient and the baby about to make its way into the world, both of whom needed her to do this. She pushed off, landing back gently further down.

'Good. Just keep going like that,' Roman encouraged from beside her with no trace of impatience, only praise.

It convinced her she could do this, taking bigger and bigger steps, confident her feet would find the rock face again each time. Seeing her progress spurred Roman to carry on down at his own pace and she wanted to keep up so she wouldn't become a hindrance to the rescue. With renewed bravado she went to push off again, but her foot slipped, her body slammed into the cliff, the jagged edges tearing at her skin and clothes. The shock caused her to let go of the rope and suddenly she was free falling, with nothing to cling to.

'Grab the rope, put the safety clip on, Sophie, before you hit the ground!' Roman was yelling from in the darkness. He didn't sound that far away and she knew she had little time to react before she slammed into the ground below.

She had several attempts to right herself before she managed to get the safety clip on and halt her rapid descent. For a while she dangled in mid-air, her rapid breath clouding the air around her.

'You're almost there. Just take it easy. I'll guide you down.' Roman was there as always, encouraging her and convincing her she could do this.

Sophie put her hand out and felt for the solid wall before pulling herself in towards it. She rested her head against the cool surface for a moment while she gathered herself together again before making the final descent.

After a couple of steps she felt a hand at

her back and Roman guided her back down onto solid ground. Her hands were shaking as she undid her harness and practically threw herself at him when she was free. It didn't matter that he had effectively dumped her only hours earlier, she needed him to hold her.

'You made it. I'm proud of you, Soph,' he mumbled into her hair, his arms wrapped around her waist and hugging her as though he didn't ever want to let go. She wished he didn't have to but there was one person who needed him more than she did.

'I did.' And she couldn't have done it without Roman's help.

Reluctantly, Sophie let go of her anchor and looked around the ledge for the person she had put her life on the line for. 'Kirstie? We're here.'

'I'm in the car!' she shouted before another pained cry pierced the night.

Using their head torches, Sophie and Roman picked their steps carefully over to the car. With the back door open, they found Kirstie lying across the back seat.

'I need to make sure the car is safe for her to be in before we do anything else.' Roman went to secure the vehicle, leaving Sophie to check on her patient.

'How are we doing, Kirstie?' she said, leaning into the car to check for any injuries.

The car interior light was dim but along with her head torch she was able to see the dirt and blood marring the young woman's face.

'I feel like I need to push,' she managed to get out through panting breaths.

'Okay, I'll take a look and see where we are.' From her preliminary observation it was mostly superficial injuries leaving Kirstie scratched and bruised. However, her body would have taken quite a battering before the vehicle had come to rest on this ledge, and possibly the baby too.

At that moment Roman came back to update her. 'We're far enough from the ledge for the car to remain stable and I've disconnected the battery to prevent the possibility of an electrical fire. I've radioed so hopefully the helicopter will be here soon to transfer the patient to the hospital.'

'Hmm. It might be too late for that. I'm just going to look and see how far along the labour is now.'

Kirstie let out another yell, the contractions coming fast.

'If you can just draw up your knees, Kirstie, I'm going to check your progress.'

Roman opened up the medical bag he'd carried down on his shoulder and Sophie took out a pair of surgical gloves. These weren't ideal sanitary conditions, but she would do the best she could to keep things sterile to prevent mother and baby contracting infection.

'Okay, you're fully dilated, Kirstie. Baby won't be long now. Roman, you'll have to tell the crew to hold off for a while. We're not going anywhere until this baby gets here.' While Roman went to radio in the latest update, Sophie hunkered down and prepared to deliver in one of her most unusual births to date.

'But how are we going to get out of here?' Kirstie was half crying as she tried to control her breathing. Now wasn't the time to tell her that, along with her newborn, she would have to be winched up into a helicopter. There was no need to further stress a woman in labour when she had other things to worry about.

'You leave that down to us.' Roman was back, adjusting the front seats to give Sophie more room to work in the back of the car. He was always thinking ahead. Something which was great for the work he did but not so good for anyone wishing to have a relationship with him.

'My labour bag is in the boot of the car,' Kirstie suddenly remembered and Roman immediately went to retrieve it.

'That's very organised of you, or were you already in labour when you set out this evening?' Kirstie was on her own, her boyfriend not prepared to settle down into family life, so she'd had to do everything alone so far during the pregnancy. Sophie supposed she should think herself lucky she hadn't been in a similar situation when Roman had decided he didn't want to be with her long-term. Although the thought of having his baby did appeal...

'I have one at work and one in the hallway at home too. I didn't want to get caught unaware.' Her laugh was interrupted by another contraction, but Sophie was glad of her overanxious mothering instincts. The bag, retrieved by Roman, contained clean towels, which she was able to spread down under Kirstie. There were nappies, baby blankets, toiletries and a change of clothes for mother and baby. Even the snacks would come in handy between now and the transfer to the hospital. Everything needed to make the pair comfortable and warm after the birth. All

Sophie had to do was make sure it all went smoothly. No pressure at all.

She thought of the journey she had just been on, of Roman who was by her side, and knew they would get through this.

'Okay, Kirstie, I can see the baby's head. With the next contraction I need you to push. That's it.' The miracle of birth would never cease to amaze Sophie as she watched the baby emerge with Kirstie's efforts, her screams echoing in the air.

'I know you're exhausted, honey, but we just need that last effort to get baby here.'

Kirstie let out an almighty roar as she pushed, and the baby slipped out into Sophie's arms. She quickly clamped the cord and wrapped the little girl in one of the blankets.

'Congratulations, Mum. You have a daughter.' Sophie had tears in her eyes too as Kirstie burst into happy, relieved sobs.

'I'll take her and get her cleaned up.' Roman had some cotton wool and a bottle of water ready as he took the crying infant from her arms. There was something poignant in that moment between them as they looked at the baby and at each other. A reminder of everything they could have had together if the past hadn't scarred them both so deeply.

It was bittersweet to see him cradling a baby so gently, being so caring and compassionate to that tiny stranger when he couldn't do the same for her, or himself. Her heart was broken all over again, watching a scene which would never be in their future. Fate was stabbing her with one last dagger to the soul.

'Can I hold her?' The mother's plea halted Sophie's self-pity and prompted her back to her midwifery skills.

'As soon as we finish here. I just need to deliver the placenta and make sure you're ready to be transferred to the hospital.'

Once all necessary examinations had been completed, Roman handed the baby over so mother and daughter could have some skin-to-skin contact.

'We don't need anyone else, do we, sweetheart?' Kirstie murmured to the little bundle curled contentedly on her chest.

Sophie envied that bond she would likely never have with another human being. Unconditional love. Even Roman had come with strings attached—don't fall in love, don't ask him to stay and definitely don't go and see his parents behind his back to try and reconcile them. She was doomed to be on her own for the rest of her life. Kirstie didn't realise how lucky she was to have someone, to have a family.

'If we're ready I'll radio in for transfer. We don't want anyone out in the cold for too long.' Roman reminded them that this was no warm, cosy delivery suite but the edge of a cliff face at the very end of November. Kirstie and the little one were vulnerable and needed to get somewhere safe as soon as possible.

They all set to work getting mother and baby dressed and ready to be transported. Sophie was trying not to think about how she was going to get back onto solid ground in case her look of panic set Kirstie off too. The idea of winching a newborn up into a helicopter wasn't for the faint-hearted.

She couldn't believe any of this was happening as the helicopter came into view above them, lights shining, blades whirring and the wind whipping around them. It was all the drama she'd never wanted in her life but it had come to her unbidden and she had got through it. The baby certainly hadn't asked to be brought into this world in this manner. Fate, it seemed, paid no mind to plans and precautions.

Roman's colleagues took over responsibility for her patients from the moment they lowered themselves down on ropes from the helicopter, lifting mother and baby to relative safety. It was only when the crew flew off into the night, plunging Sophie and Roman back into relative darkness, that the implications of her position became apparent. Stranded on a ledge with her ex at night.

'Er…how are we supposed to get back?' There was a lot of other deeply personal stuff she wanted to say to him but probably not here where she couldn't get away from him when he said something she didn't want to hear. She was already tired and emotional without being reminded of her failings as a potential partner.

He handed her the climbing gear she'd hoped to have seen for the last time when she had taken it off earlier. 'What comes down must go up again.'

'I don't think that's a thing. Tell me you're kidding me, right?' Sophie glanced up at the sheer face of the cliff as far as the eye and head torch could reach. The top seemed even further away from this angle.

'Nope. They don't have the time or resources to come back out just for us. Someone will come and pick us up at the top in a support vehicle. You've done it already. There's nothing to it. You'll just have to follow my path and footholds on the way.' He made it sound as though they were going picking wildflowers, not climbing rocks in the dark.

'Easy-peasy,' she said with a shrug, hoping he could see her eyes rolling at him in the light of his torch.

'I know you can do it, Soph. I've just seen you abseil down a cliff and deliver a baby in the back seat of a car. You're a real-life superwoman.'

But still not enough to convince Roman that he wanted to be with her.

'Yeah? In that case could you tell the powers that be I'd really appreciate a pair of wings or a flying cape to get me to the top?' It wasn't as if she had any choice but to start climbing or she would be stuck down here all night and she really wanted to get home to her bed. Even if it would be on her own for the first time in weeks.

'You've done the hard part. Come on, I'll give you a leg up.' Once Roman had given her all the necessary safety checks and brief instructions on how to make her ascent, Sophie knew there were no more excuses.

She gripped onto the rocks and found

her first foothold before Roman gave her a boost up off the ground. It wasn't an easy climb and took twice as long as her earlier descent. The fine rain falling and misting everything in its path didn't help, making the surface slippery under her feet. A few times she lost her footing, her knees and shins taking a battering in the process. But Roman was there for her every step of the way, encouraging and pushing her, sometimes literally, to get her to the finish line. By the time she reached the top every part of her was shaking from the cold and exertion of getting there.

Roman took off his safety gear and came to her, wrapping her in his arms and instantly providing some heat. Everything seemed to hit her at once. The drama of the birth, the adrenaline of her climb and the sheer heartbreak of being with Roman and knowing it could be the last time. She broke down and sobbed into his chest.

'You did so well, Soph. I'm really proud of you.' He was making this so much harder for her with his kind words and hugs and, really, he was lucky she didn't push him back over that cliff.

When the support car came to collect them and caught their embrace in its headlights she quickly let go. It was bad enough Roman had witnessed her breakdown and total inability to accept their situation without anyone else seeing it. They got into the car and both were swathed in emergency foil blankets to keep them warm.

'I suppose you'll want to get home to bed after all that excitement.' Roman was trying to make small talk with her in the back of the car.

She thought about the dark empty cottage and the ghosts waiting for her there. 'No, I want to be dropped off at the hospital to see how Kirstie and the baby are doing.'

'I thought you might.' He grinned but it irked her that he knew her better than she knew herself.

'There's no need for you to attend. She's my patient. Feel free to get dropped off at your place first.' Sophie was not putting him under any obligation to spend any more time with her. He must be desperate to make an escape after tonight's unexpected turn. It was always awkward when you dumped someone then had to spend the rest of the night together on an emergency medical call out delivering a baby on a cliff edge.

'No, I want to go. I prefer to see my patients right through their transfer, so I know everything was done properly.'

Sophie wasn't going to argue with him. If he was trying to make a point he could make it and then go home, and she could start getting used to the idea that he would no longer be in her life.

As the car jostled along the coast road Sophie rested her head against the window, watching the distant waves continuing to crash as though nothing had happened tonight. As her eyes began to flutter closed she wondered if she could ever be as unaffected by the world around her as the sea.

CHAPTER EIGHT

ROMAN WATCHED SOPHIE SLEEP. He didn't rouse her even though he had so much he needed to say. She deserved her rest when he knew what the past few hours had taken out of her, and not just physically. She had faced her fears head-on, tackled them mostly without complaint. Her bravery put him to shame when he had run away from his rather than risk getting hurt. Despite him ending their relationship earlier in the evening, she had set aside her own personal issues to work alongside him, doing whatever it took to keep her patient safe. Including risking her life, a feat he was sure she didn't undertake lightly, given the fears which had plagued her since her parents' death.

Working with an ex, abseiling down a cliff in the dark and delivering a baby in a car...and he couldn't even tell a woman he loved her. Afraid of committing in case he wasn't enough for her and somewhere along the line she told him so. Roman wasn't the daredevil everyone believed him to be. He was a coward.

When they reached the hospital he was forced to wake her, giving her a gentle shake. 'Sophie? We're here. Are you sure you wouldn't rather go home to bed? I can call in and let you know how they're doing later if you've changed your mind.'

At the very suggestion she bolted upright, defying that she was in any way tired. 'No. I won't sleep until I know they're doing okay.'

After watching her fall into such a deep sleep so quickly he doubted it. She was clearly exhausted. But Roman didn't wish to cause her any embarrassment or cause a row between them. Regardless of everything, he didn't wish them to part on bad terms.

He opened the car door for her and she did accept his hand when he offered to help her out. Mostly, he suspected, because her legs were a little wobbly after the night's events.

'When you get home you should make yourself a stiff drink and run a bath to ease those muscles.'

'I know how to look after myself, thank you.'

He regretted attempting to tell her what to

do when she snatched her hand away again. She marched up to the reception desk, back ramrod-straight, giving nothing away about how weary she must be, and enquired about her patient.

'Oh, you're the pair who rescued her? You're a couple of heroes around here.' The young receptionist stood up, drawing attention to them from the few people in the waiting room.

'Just doing our jobs. Now, if we could see her...' Sophie batted away the praise as easily as she had deflected Roman's concerns. He could see her defences already rebuilding brick by brick and it was sad to see when she had been so open with him. His fault for letting her believe they could have a future together and leaving it too late to tell her otherwise. Of course it had always been on the cards, he'd been foolish to think otherwise. Sophie wasn't one to hold back her emotions the way he did, but he had selfishly not wanted to end things when he'd enjoyed being with her so much.

His life was spent hopping from one job, one town, one short-lived relationship to the next and he had never been as truly happy as he had with Sophie. Whatever time they had together surely was better than the nomadic life he'd been leading since the day he'd left home? But as she marched ahead with no desire to wait for him Roman wondered if he had left it too late to fix his mistake.

He decided to give her some space before he attempted a grovelling apology and took the elevator to the cardiac care unit to see his father.

'Hello, Roman.' His mother was sitting by his father's bedside, holding his hand.

'I thought I would call in and see how you were feeling, Dad.'

'Sore,' he managed to get out from behind his oxygen mask.

'I'm sure you are. Sorry if I was too heavy-handed.' Bruised or even cracked ribs were often the result of chest compressions, even though it was necessary to press down hard to keep the blood pumping around the body.

'You did what you had to, to save your father, and we're both very grateful.' The crack in his mother's voice and her usual composure said how thankful she was to still have her husband here, no matter how poorly he remained.

'Just doing my job,' he said, hoping they realised now how important it was to have medical professionals like him in an emergency.

'What about Sophie? Is she all right? She's such a lovely woman. Give her our apologies for the way we may have spoken to her.' Despite his mother saying all the right things about Sophie, Roman was stuck on the last part of the comment. She hadn't mentioned getting a bad reception as such, but he could imagine the disdain with which she might have been treated. Sophie didn't deserve any ill treatment when she had gone there to try and smooth things over between them. Yet again she had been the innocent victim in the fallout of his disastrous personal life.

'Sophie's fine. It was one of her patients who was in trouble. What did you say to her?'

'You know your father. He wasn't in the best of moods and he doesn't like being told what to do.' His mother tried to excuse her husband's behaviour and not for the first time. Too often she had been complicit in his berating of Roman too, sometimes joining in, giving opinions he wasn't sure were hers or his father's. Still, neither of them had gone out of their way to stop him leaving home a decade ago.

'That's not a reason to be rude to the woman I love. I don't care what you think about me, but please, never speak to Sophie the way you ever did to me.' Roman was aware he had used the 'L' word and said it to the wrong person. It was wasted on his parents, and it was Sophie who deserved to hear it from him first. Even if she rejected it and him.

'We are sorry, son,' his mother reiterated, uncharacteristically contrite. Perhaps his father's near-death experience had made them reconsider the way they conducted themselves.

'You were outstanding tonight and the staff have been telling us about some of the other emergencies you've been involved in. It appears you're very popular around here.' Despite his obvious discomfort, his father was doing his best to make amends.

In all the scenarios which had played out in his head of meeting his parents, he had never imagined it like this. They seemed almost…human.

'And respected,' his mother added, nudging his father.

'You should rest, Dad. This can wait for another day.' Roman didn't want him to waste his energy. He'd waited a lifetime for this conversation so he was sure another few days wouldn't hurt. Except his father was waving away his concerns as per usual, stubbornly determined to have his say no matter what.

'I know we've never seen eye to eye—'

He snort-laughed at his father's understatement of the millennium.

'We will probably never agree on a number of things, but on this occasion I think we can say we were wrong.'

Edward Callahan's almost-apology was supported by a nod from his wife. Roman could only listen on in incredulous silence.

'We would have preferred you had gone into the family business like your brothers, but you've done us proud in your chosen career nonetheless.'

He was sure there was a residual barb in his father's words, but it wouldn't take away from the gesture. It was an olive branch. More than had been offered in over a decade and more than he had ever expected from them. If not for Sophie, he would never have followed up on a visit to his parents. His dad's heart attack had been the catalyst for ultimately getting them all to see sense, but it was only because of her efforts that they had even had a conversation.

As Roman had learned through many of the tragedies he saw in the nature of his work, life was short and should not be lived in bitterness, or alone.

'For the record, I think Sophie is a fantastic match for you. She's as passionate and headstrong as you always were, but her heart is in the right place.'

'Thanks. I think.' Roman's mind was whirling with the implications of this moment with his parents. Did this mean he hadn't disappointed them after all? That he was not the useless son he had been told his entire life but 'passionate and headstrong', qualities which they had struggled to accept? It didn't change who he was but perhaps the way he perceived himself when he had been so afraid of having the same toxic relationship with someone else. Now they were accepting they were to blame at the same time he had been considering making a commitment to the only woman he had ever loved. His parents seemed to have a high opinion of Sophie too, not that it mattered to him, but it took someone extra special to get their approval.

'I hope we'll get to meet her again soon. Perhaps both of you might come to dinner one night when your father is feeling better?' his mother suggested, trying again to build a bridge across the years spent apart. It could prove to be too little too late, old quarrels might raise their head again, but Roman had spent too long on his own, anticipating the very worst that could happen in any of his relationships. Sophie had shown him that sometimes you simply had to get on with things, no matter how afraid you were, and hope for the best.

'We'll see. I'll have to talk to Sophie first.' He had a lot to say to her, if she even wanted to hear it. She was more than capable of continuing her life without him in it, as she had proven time and time again.

'We just wanted to say we're sorry, son, and we're proud of you.' Roman knew exactly what it would have taken for his father to admit to being wrong. That praise was something he had wanted for his entire life but tonight it fell flat as he realised he had made mistakes too where Sophie was concerned. She was more important than celebrating a win over his parents.

'Thanks, I appreciate it. Now, you rest up. I'll call in again later, but I should go and check on Sophie.' Roman didn't know if he was going to be around for much longer to build on their budding relationship. It all depended on Sophie and whether or not she would forgive him for letting her down after all.

'Hey. How are you two doing?' Sophie poked her head around the cubicle curtain to see Kirstie sitting up in bed with her daughter cradled in her arms. There was nothing in her smile to suggest the birth had been traumatic, despite the circumstances. Sophie hoped they had managed to minimise her distress as much as possible.

'We're doing great. Thanks to you and your colleague.'

'Roman.'

'Is he here with you?'

'He was...' She'd expected him to have caught up with her now. Perhaps he had decided to wait until she had gone before visiting Kirstie to avoid any further awkwardness between them. After all, it was only a few hours ago that he had told her he didn't want to be with her any more. She should be glad he was avoiding her—except in emergency labour situations—it might make it easier for her, not seeing him and being reminded of how much she loved him.

It hurt. If she had fallen off that cliff, bounced the whole way down head first into the sea, she didn't think she would be in as much pain as she was now. Working beside him had merely reminded her of all the reasons she did love him. His support and patience getting her down the cliff, the tenderness with which he'd held the baby and the courage which he showed every day in his work. The only thing lacking in her perfect man was love for her. Something kind of important when considering a relationship. Which, clearly, he never had.

'Oh. Maybe I'll see him later. I just wanted to say thanks again to both of you. I dread to think what would have happened if you two hadn't gone out of your way to get to me.' Kirstie hugged her baby a little tighter.

'I'm sure you would have managed. You did so well out there on your own. I hope the circumstances didn't spoil the experience for you.' Sometimes a difficult birth put women off having any more children or made it hard for them to bond with their child. Although Kirstie looked totally smitten with her little girl.

'Not at all. If anything, it's made me believe we can do anything. She's a survivor like me.'

'I'm sure you'll make a great team.' Sophie loved to see parent and child bonding, but it did make her think about Roman holding the baby. Her idea of a perfect family, but one she could never hope to have.

She was about to excuse herself before she made a scene when the baby began to grizzle.

'I think someone's hungry.'

'I was going to go and let you settle anyway, Kirstie. I'll put you on my schedule for a home visit when you're ready. Goodnight.' Sophie stumbled back out into the hallway before the tears of self-pity began to fall.

'Soph?'

It was just her luck having Roman walk up to her in that moment and witness her emotional breakdown after managing to stay so strong all night. Well, most of the night, if she erased the memory of collapsing into his arms after climbing back up the cliff.

'Kirstie's just in there feeding the baby at the minute. I'm going to head home.' She put her head down, hoping he hadn't seen her crying, and hurried past him.

'Wait.' Insisting on prolonging her humiliation, Roman jogged down the corridor after her.

After deeming it too childish to ignore him and keep walking, she let out an exasperated, 'What?'

'We need to talk.'

'What else could there possibly be to say, Roman? You don't want to be with me. Fine. Let's not pretend there's anything more to it than that.'

'Don't be like that, Soph.'

'I'm not being like anything, Roman. We're not together. We never really were. You've made that abundantly clear.' There was no point in stringing this out or continuing to pretend to herself they'd had anything other than a fling. Which was exactly what she had signed up for, so it was entirely her fault she was hurting, but still, she was feeling sorry for herself and was entitled to be a little spiky in lieu of ice cream and chocolate to console herself after their breakup.

'Will you please stop stomping off and talk to me?' Roman grabbed her and dragged her into the nearest empty cubicle.

'You know, they probably need this for a patient. I don't know why—'

'I went to see my parents earlier.'

'How did that go?' Curiosity apparently had overtaken her rage as she waited for him to share the details of the encounter.

'Not so good. My father had a heart attack.'

'Oh, Roman. I'm so sorry.'

'It's okay, he's here in the hospital. I managed to bring him back.'

'I'm sure they were glad to have you there, but I'm sorry you had to go through that.'

'Yeah, well, it put a lot of things into perspective and we're back on speaking terms at least. By the way, they said to say sorry for the way they treated you and...' he took a deep breath '...told me they were proud of me.'

Her eyes must have shown her incredulity that they had expressed any positive emotion towards anyone, but especially him, after the terse conversation she'd had with them.

'I know. I think my father's brush with mortality might have made him think about his life choices. Perhaps my mother realised if she lost him she doesn't have anyone else around her.' He shrugged. 'I don't know what brought it on, but they did seem to be making an effort. Although he's that woozy from the medication I'm not sure he'll remember.'

'Your mother will remind him if it comes to it. I'm glad you finally got some acknowledgement of your accomplishments.' Sophie was happy that something good had come out of this mess after all, but it didn't change anything for her. Even if he did decide to move back permanently and make reparations with his parents, he wouldn't be doing it for her. She hadn't been enough reason for him to stay.

'People make mistakes…say things they don't mean.'

'It doesn't make the words any less painful.'

'No, but an apology and a second chance can make all the difference to both parties.'

'I guess.' She didn't know why he was saying these things to her. It was none of her business what happened between him and his parents, as he'd told her earlier.

'I want to apologise too. For what I said and for not being honest with you. I'm sorry I was too afraid of being a failure in your eyes to think we could have a future.'

'And now? What are you saying, Roman?' None of this made sense to her. Talking about his parents and apologising was all taking time away from drowning her sorrows in calories and alcohol, unless he had something better to offer her.

He made a strangled groaning noise and ran his fingers through his hair, leaving it in soft waves behind his ears. 'You'll have to excuse me. I'm not used to asking anyone to take me back or telling them I love them.'

Sophie's heart pumped a little faster, though she did appear to have stopped breathing. 'You haven't. You didn't ask me to take you back or tell me you love me. I would have noticed when they're the words I've been waiting to hear from you for a lifetime.'

If he was really going to lay out all of his emotions in this cubicle, she would do the same. Although her revelation might not come as much of a shock as Roman's. Could it really be true? She didn't dare hope, through fear of being the victim of a cruel joke.

Roman took her hands in his and fixed her under his brown-eyed gaze to ensure she wasn't going anywhere. 'I love you. Will you take me back?'

'Not that I want to ruin the moment, but why? Only a few hours ago you were telling me the exact opposite and now I'm supposed to believe this is what you really want? What happened for you to change your mind about staying with me? Apart from a near-death experience on a cliff.' Perhaps Roman was going through the same thing as his father, thinking about his own mortality and deciding he didn't want to be alone. Whilst she wanted Roman to be in her life, she wouldn't accept anything less than real love and commitment this time. Her poor heart couldn't take any more false promises.

'It's not about what happened out there tonight. Well, I suppose it is, in a way. It just reminded me of what an amazing woman you are. I never changed my mind about the rest. I've always loved you and always wanted to be with you, but I was afraid of letting you down. I didn't want to see the same look of disappointment in your eyes that I saw in my parents' every day, when you realised I couldn't live up to your ideals.'

'But I never—'

'You never asked anything of me, I know. But in my heart I felt the weight of expectation to be everything to you your parents hadn't been. I know I've been an idiot, but if you can find it in you to forgive me maybe we could try again?'

'You're making me dizzy with the sudden turnaround, Roman.' It was difficult to accept what he was telling her now as the truth when she was still hurting from his earlier rejection. Even if he was giving her his best puppy impression.

'I always wanted to be with you, but what we've had together has been so good it terrified me. It made me think we couldn't possibly sustain it past Christmas. That I couldn't be the person you need to make you happy. I'm truly sorry for hurting you and I understand if you don't ever want to see me again. All I want is for you to be happy and in my twisted logic it made sense that I left and let you move on.'

Now that Roman had explained his behaviour there was a bud of hope blossoming in Sophie's soul that all wasn't lost after all. Her heart had been broken when she'd thought she would have to face life without Roman again and though things weren't perfect and they had a lot to learn about communicating their emotions, working through their problems was preferable to another separation.

'Haven't you learned anything? It's never better for me when you leave.' She slid her arms around Roman's waist, wanting to hold him close and remind them both of what they had together.

'Nor me. Perhaps it's time I stopped thinking about the worst that could happen, to concentrate on the here and now.' The look of love was there in Roman's eyes as he gazed down at her, in the warmth and strength of his embrace as he held her, and for once he was recognising it. There was only one thing left for him to do if they were going to have a future and that was to make a commitment. Something he had been running from for over ten years.

'Never mind doing what you think is right for others, what is it you want, Roman?'

'You.'

'Right answer,' she said, making them both smile.

'Apparently you meet with my parents' approval too.'

'I'm so glad.' There was more than a hint of sarcasm in her voice.

'It's got me thinking that maybe I could be a good long-term partner for you too, if you would give me the chance? What do you say about getting hitched, Soph?' he asked with a lopsided smile that made her question if he was being totally serious.

'As much as I've longed for this moment to happen some day, I didn't anticipate such a casual proposal.' Sophie was trying, and failing, to control her haywire pulse, unable to believe that this was happening. Afraid to buy into it too quickly, only to crash back down to earth when it turned out not to be her fairy tale ending.

Roman frowned, marking the end of the so-called happy occasion. 'Is that a no?'

'Roman, I don't want you to ask me because you think it's what I want or what your parents want. It has to be something that comes from your heart. I can't risk you changing your mind and abandoning me somewhere down the line. I would rather be on my own than be with you if you didn't love me. I need to know you're serious.'

'I'm completely serious. I've told you I love you. I always have and always will, Sophie. I was ready to make a commitment to you before we even went down that cliff because I missed you so much. And seeing you face your fears so bravely only strengthened my resolve to do the same. None of my decisions were ever about not wanting to be with you but because I was afraid of ruining things between us. Meeting my parents tonight, hearing them say they were proud of me was simply the icing on an already special night. I just wanted to make things official so we can stop questioning if we have a future together. We can wait as long as you like, or we don't have to get engaged now if I need to prove my commitment to you first. I simply need you to know I'm yours for keeps.'

She knew the gesture was so much more than a spur-of-the-moment decision when he was telling her everything she had ever wanted. Roman had never promised her anything more than he was willing to give, and she was aware how significant a lifetime commitment was for him. Now it was her turn to be brave and believe they could finally have a future together instead of hiding away from the world for the rest of her life. It was time for her to start living without fear.

'You don't need to prove anything more to me, Roman. I trust you.'

'In that case, Sophie French, will you do me the honour of becoming my wife?' Roman got down on one knee and, despite the sterile environment around them and the smell of disinfectant, Sophie thought it the most romantic moment of her entire life.

'Yes, Roman Callahan, I will marry you.' Being with him had taught her to take a few risks now and then and she thought this was one worth taking.

Everything they had gone through together had been leading to this moment, making every second of their separation and her heartache worth it for them to realise how much they needed each other. It was perfect. All of it.

EPILOGUE

Three years later

SOPHIE EASED HERSELF into the front seat of the car and waved to Penelope and Edward until they disappeared back inside their house. 'Phew, I'm glad that's over. No offence, Roman, but I can only take your family in small doses. Especially on Christmas Day. I just want to get home to our own place and veg out in front of the TV for a while.'

Roman finished clipping Freddie into his car seat in the back before getting into the driving seat. 'Me too. Now you know why I preferred being at the cottage with you and your gran when I was younger.'

She understood very well now that she had experience of being in the company of Roman's family. Deep down, Sophie knew they were good people, but neither she nor Roman were able to fully relax around them. He and his dad always clashed over something, today over letting Freddie open his presents before they went to church. The Callahan family tradition of unwrapping gifts apparently meant he should have waited until after the service. However, Roman had been quick to point out *their* new family tradition was completely different. They weren't going to stifle Freddie's joy on Christmas morning. If they were honest, she was sure she and Roman had been equally excited to see him open his presents under the tree, even if at eighteen months old he wasn't entirely aware of what was going on.

Nonetheless, they were family and they loved Freddie. A mutual feeling when he showered them often with wet kisses and they didn't even complain when he put his sticky hands on their expensive clothes.

'Boys will be boys,' was often the response, which always made Roman roll his eyes. Although he was happy they were making better grandparents than parents, for his son's sake. Sophie was on tenterhooks on their visits, unused to such grandeur and with a toddler let loose in the vast space she was always worried he would cause some catastrophe. Roman, as always, was the one to calm her down and reassure her their son was simply exploring and couldn't be wrapped in cotton wool for ever.

For sure, they were all happiest at home in the cottage. Which, though often messy and chaotic, was full of love.

'Are you sure you don't mind if I go on this hiking holiday without you next week? I can cancel if you would prefer for me to be at home in the New Year?'

'It's fine. As long as you're careful.' She would always worry when Roman went off on his adventures, but she had accepted that his love of life was who he was and she couldn't take that away from him. Besides, he always made it up to her by taking her on a lovely, relaxing holiday in the sun. After their wedding two and a half years ago they had spent a particularly luxurious fortnight in the Bahamas, during which he had persuaded her to do some scuba diving.

'I will be careful. I've got too much to lose.' He lifted her hand and kissed it.

'I'd go with you but you know—' She nodded towards the bump, which was becoming noticeably bigger these days. Even her fingers were getting fatter, and she'd had to take off her wedding and engagement rings, something she hated having to do when they held such sentimental attachment for both of them.

The engagement ring was a family tradition Roman's mother had saved especially for him. The exquisite diamond had been his grandmother's and Penny Callahan had reserved it for her youngest son, in the hope he would eventually come back into the family fold. The significance had not been lost on either of them. Sophie treasured it, along with the wedding ring she had picked out with Roman on a romantic trip to Paris he'd surprised her with to celebrate their engagement. Until her body was hers again, Sophie would have to hold onto the memories alone.

'Maybe next year we'll think about having Christmas dinner at home. You know, start a new Callahan tradition.' It was his excuse for doing things his parents didn't approve of and seemed to be working fine so far. His parents could see what a great father he was and had no reason to criticise him in that area at least.

'I like the sound of that. Especially when we'll have two small children to handle.' She liked the idea of the cottage on Christmas morning, full of toys and chaos and a family happy to be spending time together. Just as she had always imagined it.

* * * * *

*If you missed the previous story in
the Carey Coves Midwives quartet,
then check out*

Christmas with the Single Dad Doc
by Annie O'Neil

*If you enjoyed this story, check out these
other great reads from Karin Baine*

**A GP to Steal His Heart
Wed for Their One Night Baby
The Nurse's Christmas Hero**

All available now!